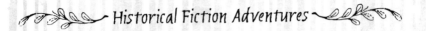

The Lucky Baseball

My Story in a Japanese-American Internment Camp

Suzanne Lieurance

Enslow Publishers, Inc.
40 Industrial Road
Box 398
Berkeley Heights, NJ 07922
USA

http://www.enslow.com

J
FIC
LIE

gr. 5-7
(20)

This book is a work of fiction. References to real people, events, establishments, organizations, or locales are intended only to provide a sense of authenticity, and are used to advance the fictional narrative. All other characters, and all incidents and dialogue, are drawn from the author's imagination and are not to be construed as real.

Library of Congress Cataloging-in-Publication Data:

Lieurance, Suzanne.
    The lucky baseball : my story in a Japanese-American internment camp / Suzanne Lieurance.
        p. cm. — (Historical fiction adventures (HFA))
    Summary: In 1942 after the Japanese bomb Pearl Harbor, twelve-year-old Harry Yakamoto and his family are forced to move to an internment camp where they must learn to survive in the desert of California under the watch of armed guards. Includes section about the treatment of Japanese Americans during World War II.
    Includes bibliographical references.
    ISBN-13: 978-0-7660-3311-5
    ISBN-10: 0-7660-3311-2
    1. Japanese Americans—Evacuation and relocation, 1942-1945—Juvenile fiction.
2. Manzanar War Relocation Center—Juvenile fiction. 3. World War, 1939–1945—United States—Juvenile fiction. [1. Japanese Americans—Evacuation and relocation, 1942-1945—Fiction. 2. Manzanar War Relocation Center—Fiction. 3. Baseball—Fiction. 4. World War, 1939–1945—United States—Fiction.] I. Title.
    PZ7.L6194Lu 2009
    [Fic]—dc22   2009001379

ISBN-13: 978-0-7660-3655-0 (paperback)
ISBN-10: 0-7660-3655-5 (paperback)

Printed in the United States of America

10 9 8 7 6 5 4 3 2 1

To Our Readers: We have done our best to make sure all Internet Addresses in this book were active and appropriate when we went to press. However, the author and the publisher have no control over and assume no liability for the material available on those Internet sites or on other Web sites they may link to. Any comments or suggestions can be sent by e-mail to comments@ enslow.com or to the address on the back cover.

Illustration Credits: Franklin D. Roosevelt Presidential Library, p. 154; Library of Congress, pp. 156, 158; National Archives and Records Administration, p. 155; Original Painting by © Corey Wolfe, p. 1.

Cover Illustration: Original Painting by © Corey Wolfe.

Contents

chapter one

The Bully of Seven Cedars

It was an ordinary December afternoon in 1941 in Seven Cedars, California. My best friend, Mike Nagasawa, and I headed for the big dirt field in town called Kramer's Lot, where all the local kids played baseball. When we got there we saw Tony Rossi and his friends. They were such sheep. They followed Tony everywhere and did whatever he told them to do.

Tony told them not to play baseball with Mike or me. Because they would not let us play, Mike and I never got to play an actual baseball game with a full set of players. A few kids in the neighborhood would stand up to Tony and play with us. But there were never enough to make up two complete teams. Tony also encouraged his friends to hurl insults at us whenever possible. So Mike and I always stayed as far away from Tony and his bunch as we could— on the opposite side of the field.

I wound up for a fastball (not my best pitch, but I was working on it) while Mike stood waiting for it, his old baseball bat held securely over his shoulder. I released the ball, and Mike got ready to swing. When he did, Tony's boys whistled so loudly they startled Mike, and he missed the ball.

The boys booed, then laughed and whistled.

I heard Tony Rossi say, "See? What did I tell you? Japs can't play baseball."

I wanted to run over and punch Tony in the nose. But Mike threw down the bat, hurried over, and held me by the shoulders. "Let it go, Harry," he said. "Tony's a jerk and everybody knows it."

Mike was right about that. Tony Rossi was the biggest jerk in all of Southern California, not just Seven Cedars, as far as I was concerned. But knowing that didn't make me feel any better. Still, if I got into a fight with Tony, and Papa found out about it, I'd be in big trouble. Besides, with all of Tony's friends surrounding him, it wouldn't be a fair fight anyway. I knew that, and Mike knew it. That's why I picked up the baseball and said, "Let's get out of here."

Mike grabbed his bat and we hopped on our bikes as Tony and his gang shouted a few more insults across the dirt field.

Someday I'll show you guys, I thought, as we rode off for home. But all I wanted was to fit in with all the other kids in Seven Cedars. Mike probably did, too, although he would never admit it to anyone—even to me. He pedaled along beside me now, his baseball bat stretched out over his handlebars.

"I'm so sick of those guys," he said. "We'll never get any good at baseball if they won't stop bothering us while we're trying to practice."

"I guess that's the point," I said. "They're afraid we'll be better players than they are, and they couldn't stand to see that happen."

"Why do they hate us so much?" Mike asked. "We're Japanese, so what? We never did anything bad to them."

I stood up on the bike to pedal uphill. "We're not Japanese," I corrected him. "We're Americans, just like they are. We were born in this country. We look a little different from Tony and his friends, that's all."

We came to the top of the hill. We were both huffing and puffing, but now Mike and I stopped pedaling and coasted alongside each other.

Mike took a deep breath. "Well, I wish people didn't dislike us because of the way we look," he said.

"It could be worse," I answered.

But I had no idea how bad things were about to get.

chapter two

A Grand Prize

When I woke up the very next morning, I'd forgotten all about what had happened with Tony Rossi the day before. I just knew it was going to be a great day. Of course, the fact that it was Saturday—the day for the big prize drawing at Weaver's General Store—had a lot to do with the way I was feeling. I had entered that drawing so many times that I was just sure Mr. Weaver would be pulling a slip of paper with my name on it out of the barrel of contest entries. Unlike most of the other people living in Seven Cedars, Mr. Weaver was nice to me. And he was fair and honest, so I knew he wouldn't rig the contest.

There was one catch. I had to be at the store during the drawing in order to win. If I wasn't there, then Mr. Weaver would draw another name from the brown barrel. Then that person would win the prize I had been dreaming about for so many weeks.

I tucked my shirttail into the waist of my pants, tied my shoes, then pulled on my favorite baseball cap. I charged out of my room.

We lived in a small apartment over the restaurant my grandparents had opened many years ago when they came to this country from Japan. My father had been about twelve years old at the time—just like I am now. He grew up working in the restaurant. When he married my mother, she worked with him until she got sick. She died soon after I was born. Now Papa was in charge of the business, but my grandparents still worked there, and they lived with Papa and me.

I had almost made it to the front door when Papa yelled out from the kitchen, "Just where do you think you're going, young man?"

I froze. Then I pulled off the cap before Papa caught me wearing a hat in the house. "Today's the drawing, Papa. I have to be at Weaver's at noon. If Mr. Weaver draws my name and I'm not there, I'll lose the prize."

Papa walked into the living room. He puffed on his pipe and stared at me over the small black-rimmed glasses perched on his nose. A little ring of smoke hung in the air above him. "Hmpf," he snorted. "It's not like you need another baseball. You already have dozens of them."

"But this baseball is special, Papa. You know that."

Papa took another puff of his pipe. Finally, he said, "And I'm sure you and Mike will want to go to Kramer's Lot to play baseball after the drawing." He studied me for a few seconds. "All right, go. But be back by four o'clock. Restaurants don't run themselves, you know."

I smiled. "Thanks, Papa. I'll be back by four o'clock. I promise."

I ran for the front door and was down the outside stairs before Papa had time to change his mind. As soon as I was on the sidewalk, I slapped my baseball cap back on my head and ran around to the back alley.

Mike was standing beside his bike waiting for me. "What took you so long? We're gonna be late."

"No, we aren't!" I said. Then I noticed Mike's little sister, Mary. Lately, she tagged along with us every chance she got. "What's she doing here?"

Mary was wearing a baseball cap, too. She made goo-goo eyes at me and smiled.

I wanted to puke. Out of all the boys in Seven Cedars, Mary just had to have a crush on me.

"Hi, Harry," she said sweetly.

I ignored her and unchained my bike from the fence behind the alley, then grabbed the handlebars and took off running. As soon as I picked up a little speed, I jumped on and pedaled as fast as I could.

"Race you there!" I yelled back to Mike, who was still standing there.

He lifted Mary onto the handlebars of his bike. Then he jumped on the seat himself and struggled to catch up with me.

It was only three blocks to Weaver's, so it didn't take us long to get there. Bicycles were lined up on the sidewalk in front of the store. We parked ours with the rest of them, then went inside. Weaver's always smelled like new leather, fertilizer, and spices. Mr. Weaver stood behind a big barrel filled with tiny slips of paper. A full-size cardboard cutout of Joe DiMaggio—the best baseball player to ever live—stood next to Mr. Weaver. Boys of all ages were jammed into the spaces between aisles of merchandise as well as the small space in front of Mr. Weaver. A few girls and some grown-ups were there, too.

Someone rang an old school bell to get the crowd's attention.

Mr. Weaver cleared his throat loudly and said, "Hello, everyone, and welcome. It's wonderful to see so many of you here today for the drawing of our grand prize in the Take Me Out to the Ball Game contest."

I felt a hard poke in the back, then Tony Rossi whispered in my ear, "Sorry," as if he didn't mean to poke me on purpose. For some reason, he always let me know when he was around, and he would appear out of nowhere. I guess he just wanted me to realize he was always watching me.

I frowned and pulled away from him.

Mr. Weaver dug his hand into the barrel and wiggled it around among all the slips of paper. Finally, he grabbed one of them and pulled his hand out.

I felt my heart pound. I took a deep breath and crossed my fingers for luck.

Mr. Weaver unfolded the slip of paper and looked at it, then smiled at the crowd. "Ladies and gentlemen, we have a winner."

Billy Rogers, the drummer for the marching band at Seven Cedars High School, was there with his snare drum. Mr. Weaver always liked to create as much excitement and interest in his store as possible. He constantly sponsored contests like this one and had Billy play his drum or another band member play the trumpet or trombone.

Billy gave a little roll on the drum. I could tell that every boy in the store was holding his breath.

"And the winner is . . ."

Mr. Weaver scanned the room, trying to drag out the announcement until we all burst with anticipation.

I thought I was going to pass out. I needed to take a breath, but I just couldn't. Not yet.

"Harry Yakamoto!" he said at last.

The room was silent for a split second before a few people applauded. Most of the boys in the store didn't say anything at all. Although I did hear more than one person say, "Ahh . . . shoot!"

Mike slapped me on the back and yelled out, "Yahoo! Way to go, Harry!"

Mary rushed up and hugged me so hard I thought my ribs would crack. She was strong for such a little thing. "Congratulations, Harry! You won! You won the prize!" she shouted.

I pried her off of me.

Mr. Weaver looked around the room. "There you are, Harry. Come on up here and accept your prize."

Mike shoved me toward the front of the store.

Mr. Weaver grabbed my hand and shook it. He took a red leather case containing the baseball and handed it to me just as a bright light flashed.

"Stand here and face the camera with me, Harry. We want to get a nice shot for tomorrow's newspaper."

Mr. Weaver pulled me closer to him and smiled at the man with the camera. I tried to smile, too, but my mouth didn't want to cooperate. It felt like it was full of cotton.

As I stared into the camera, the light flashed again, then Mr. Weaver said, "Congratulations, young man! For anyone here who might not know it, this baseball is autographed by none other than the great Joe DiMaggio." Mr. Weaver patted me on the back. "And Harry, I have an added surprise today."

I stared at him. "Huh?" I asked.

Mr. Weaver pulled a white envelope from his jacket pocket.

"Yes, you are one lucky young man, Harry. Your prize also includes this special invitation to meet Joe DiMaggio in person when he comes to L.A. next summer."

Now I knew I was going to pass out. A chance to meet Joe DiMaggio? In person? That would be my greatest dream come true!

Mr. Weaver placed the envelope in my hands and the photographer snapped another picture. Tony Rossi and his friends each gave me a dirty look, then they left the store.

I finally thanked Mr. Weaver for the prize. Once I started breathing normally again, I even managed a faint smile for one more picture. That seemed to satisfy the photographer, because he stopped setting off those flashes that nearly blinded me.

After I'd read the letter of invitation from Joe DiMaggio, I put it back in the envelope, then carefully placed the envelope in my pocket.

I thanked Mr. Weaver one more time, then Mike, Mary, and I ran outside, grabbed our bikes, and headed for Kramer's Lot. I clutched the red leather case to my chest and rode all the way there with just one hand on the handlebars.

Once we were at Kramer's Lot, we didn't play baseball for a while. I read the letter from Joe DiMaggio out loud to Mike and Mary, while they admired the baseball. I let them each take it out of the case and hold it for a few minutes. Then I put it back in the case, along with the letter, and set the case on the ground next to my bike.

The three of us practiced pitching and catching for a while with one of Mike's old baseballs. I had a hard time concentrating, though, because I was trying to keep an eye on that baseball case. I didn't want anyone to sneak up and take it while I wasn't looking.

I was about to pitch the ball to Mike when I suddenly thought about Papa.

"Holy smokes!" I blurted out. "Papa is waiting for me. It's almost four o'clock. I've got to get home, Mike." I tossed the ball to him.

"Okay," he said. "See ya later."

I picked up the baseball case, jumped on my bike, and raced for home.

When I got to our building, I bounded up the stairs to find Papa. But he wasn't there.

I put the baseball case in my dresser drawer where it would be safe. Then I went downstairs to help Papa.

Even before I opened the kitchen door of the restaurant, I recognized the smell of Grandmother's fried chicken. Years ago, when they'd first opened this restaurant, the menu included only Japanese foods. But my grandparents soon discovered there weren't many Japanese living in Seven Cedars—at least not many Japanese who ate out at restaurants. The people who did eat at restaurants were mostly whites, and they didn't want Japanese food. They wanted American food. Things like fried chicken and potato salad, mashed potatoes and gravy, or green beans cooked in a little bacon grease with a few bits of crispy bacon crumbled on top. And to the folks in Seven Cedars, nothing was more American than apple pie and ice cream, banana pudding, and chocolate layer cake.

It just so happened that these were the very foods my mother had grown up eating in North Carolina. And she knew how to prepare all of them. So my grandparents changed the restaurant. They renamed it Charlotte's Place in honor of my mother, who was named after the city where she was born. Soon only my mother's recipes were served at Charlotte's Place.

My mother did most of the cooking at first. But she taught my grandmother how to prepare all those Southern dishes, too. According to Papa, my mother used to tell Grandmother that the most important ingredient in any recipe is love. And I have to admit, my grandmother always put lots of love into every dish she prepares.

Once the restaurant started serving dishes made from my mother's recipes, it attracted a good crowd almost every night. On the whole, people didn't even realize a Japanese *Issei* family owned the place. My grandparents and Papa were usually in the kitchen, making sure the food was perfect and everything went smoothly. Papa hired a manager to oversee the waitresses and busboys working out front. His name was Mack Lewis, and I think most people thought Mr. Mack, as we called him, owned Charlotte's Place.

I went to the sink and washed my hands, then tied on an apron. Grandmother was chopping vegetables while Papa stirred something in a big pot on the stove. Grandfather sat on a stool in the corner, peeling potatoes over some old newspapers. Grandfather loved to garden. Many of the vegetables we served at Charlotte's Place came from his big garden in the grassy space behind our apartment.

Papa looked up at me. "There you are. You're late."

"I'm sorry. But I won the contest, Papa! I got that baseball!"

Papa smiled weakly. "Good for you. Now fill the salt and pepper shakers," he said. "Then get some napkins from the storeroom."

Grandmother finished chopping. She walked over to me. "Baseball. Baseball. That all I hear from you. Restaurant more important. It yours someday."

I cringed. I had no intention of taking over the restaurant *ever*, even though I knew that was my family's big dream for me. My grandparents took every opportunity to tell me that in their broken English. They were both born in the small mountain town of Nikko, Japan. They had lived there all their lives until they decided to move to California. They believed America offered them great opportunities.

Papa and my grandparents were still Japanese citizens because people born in Japan weren't allowed to become citizens of the United States. They were called *Issei* in Japanese. I was the only American citizen in our family because I was born in California, which automatically made me a citizen. In Japanese, I was known as *Nisei*, a child of the *Issei*. I'd never even been to Japan. Although Grandmother kept a small Shinto altar in a corner of our living room, and she and Grandfather spoke Japanese to each other most of the time, I was American through and through. Papa was, too, even though he was an *Issei*, just like they were. Papa and I were Presbyterians like many other people in Seven Cedars—not Shinto like my grandparents.

I threw my hands in the air. "I'm going to be a baseball player, Grandmother. I'm not working in a restaurant."

"Hmpf," she said as she opened the refrigerator and took out more battered chicken pieces for frying.

Grandfather looked up from the potatoes. "Your father work hard so you have good life. You be thankful."

I nodded. "Yes, I am thankful, Grandfather." I didn't say anything else. I knew there was no use arguing with him. He and Grandmother could not understand how much I loved baseball, no matter how often I told them. Maybe someday they'd realize how I felt. But for now, I needed to help Papa because it was almost time to open Charlotte's Place for dinner.

By six thirty it was really busy. Several families with children, and some couples who were either on a date or celebrating something special like a birthday, had arrived and eaten. More people were seated, looking at the menu.

My job was to fill water glasses and bus the tables. "Bus" is a fancy way of saying I cleared the dirty dishes and put a clean tablecloth, clean silverware, and napkins on each table in between customers.

Papa did most of the cooking now that Grandmother was getting old. But she insisted on doing all of the baking. She also supervised everything to make sure Papa didn't mess up any of my mother's more complicated recipes. Grandmother also loved to put the final touches on every dish. She could pipe whipped cream around the edges of a coconut cream pie, turning it from a plain dessert into something extra special. And when she garnished a salad, she knew exactly how to jazz it up with a touch of fresh herbs that my grandfather grew in his garden.

I was clearing a table in the corner when Mr. Mack walked over to me.

"Hey, Haruki. Congratulations. I hear you won the contest at Weaver's today."

I always winced when he called me Haruki, my real name. But Mr. Mack was like family. There was no way he'd ever call me Harry like my friends and everyone else in the neighborhood did. My grandparents and my father would set him straight if he did.

I placed the last of the dirty plates from the table into a plastic tub and pulled off the soiled tablecloth. I smiled. "That's right. I won a baseball signed by Joe DiMaggio."

Mr. Mack put his arm around my shoulder. He was the reason I loved baseball so much in the first place. He'd been taking me to games ever since I was a little kid. I'd carefully studied the pitchers at these games over the years and tried to copy them. I never could quite get the technique down for a killer fastball—but I kept on trying.

"That's wonderful," he said.

He walked off, and I put a fresh tablecloth on the table and smoothed out the wrinkles. Mr. Mack ushered some people over and they sat down.

"Good evening," I said. "Welcome to Charlotte's Place. I'll be back with your water glasses in a second. Your waitress will be right over with menus."

I took the tub of dirty dishes into the kitchen and set it on a cart next to the sink with the other dirty dishes that I'd brought in earlier. At least I didn't have to wash all of them. Mr. Mack's nephew, Gerald, was the dishwasher. Although lately he was hanging around Grandmother and Papa when they were cooking and baking. Like now. Grandmother was putting the finishing touches on some meatloaf. Gerald watched her like his life depended on knowing exactly how she did it.

"Gerald! Better get these dishes washed. They're starting to stack up."

Gerald looked up from the meatloaf. "Oh, yeah . . . right," he said. He walked over to the cart and took some of the dirty dishes out of the tub. He put them into the sink and began washing them.

"It's really busy out there," I said. "I'll have more dishes for you in a minute."

"I'll be ready for them," Gerald said. "Someday I'm going to be a cook, though. I don't plan on washing dishes forever, you know."

I shrugged. "If you say so."

Gerald was still a teenager, although he'd turn twenty in a few months. Still, I couldn't quite imagine him as a cook in a restaurant. I'd never seen him cook anything more complicated than a fried-egg sandwich. Even that didn't look very tasty.

I grabbed more clean napkins and another tablecloth from the storeroom and went back out to prepare another table for dinner.

Business had been slow for the past few months. Most people weren't eating out right now. They were afraid money would get really tight if the United States entered the war. But tonight they must have decided they deserved something special, because the place was packed. Every table was full and people were lined up out front.

I looked up to see Papa smiling at me. "Business is good, Haruki. I'm proud of you. And just think . . . all this

will be yours someday. If you're as fortunate as I am, you'll have a son who can work with you, just as I do."

I forced a smile. "All this," as Papa put it, was the last thing I wanted. Why couldn't my family understand that I was going to be a professional baseball player someday, and that I didn't want to run this restaurant?

chapter three

Enemy Faces

On Monday morning I woke up a few minutes before my alarm went off. I got out of bed and took the autographed baseball out of my drawer. Then I climbed back into bed and pulled the covers up to my chin. I lay there admiring Joe DiMaggio's signature. I wondered if any of the kids at school would ask me about the baseball. Probably not. I didn't have many friends. Most of my classmates usually ignored me because they were just like Tony. They didn't like *Nisei*, no matter how nice or friendly we might be.

When I finally got out of bed, I found a piece of paper and a pen and practiced my signature. Harry Yakamoto would take up a lot of space on a baseball. But it was a name people would remember.

Later, at school during recess, several boys came rushing up to ask if I had brought the baseball to school with me. I hadn't, of course. The baseball was safe in my dresser drawer at home.

Tony and his best friend, Mario, spotted Mike and me next to the swings. Tony walked over. "So, Harry, would you and Mike like to try out for our neighborhood baseball team? We could use a few new players."

Mike and I stared at each other. I knew we were both wondering why Tony was being nice to us. This had never happened before.

Then I realized what was going on. The autographed baseball, of course. Tony was being nice to us in the hopes of somehow getting his hands on my new baseball.

Mike stepped closer to Tony. "Now, why would we want to do that?" he sneered. "Japs can't play baseball. Remember?"

I interrupted before Mike could say anything else. "Hold on, Mike."

I looked at Tony. "Okay . . . we will try out for your team."

Mike stared at me like he thought I was crazy.

"We'll prove that we can play baseball," I continued. "When do we try out?"

Tony's blue eyes lit up. "Sunday, after church. Be at Kramer's Lot."

I nodded. "We'll be there."

Tony and Mario mumbled something to each other, then walked away.

Mike shook his head. "Are you crazy? Why did you tell them we'll try out for their team?"

I dug my toe in the dirt. "Relax," I said. "I figure they're just being nice to us because they think they can get me to give up that Joe DiMaggio baseball. But they're wrong about that. Still, we can try out for their team and finally prove that we are just as good as they are at baseball—no matter what we look like."

Mike shrugged. "If you say so, but I still think this is a crazy idea."

The rest of that day my mind was on baseball. I'd be doing some math problems, or looking up something in my history book, and then suddenly remember that Mike and I were going to try out for Tony's team. It wasn't a big deal. The team wasn't official. After all, it was only December—baseball season did not start for months. However, Seven Cedars wasn't the most exciting town in the country. We had a movie theater and a bowling alley. But most of us kids couldn't afford to see a movie or go bowling that often. So we played baseball all year long because it was free—and it was fun.

On Sunday, Mike and I would finally get our big chance. If we made Tony's team, maybe no one would care that we were Japanese. Maybe we'd finally be accepted as part of the gang, like all the other kids.

On Sunday afternoon, Mike and I walked over to Kramer's Lot. Mike had managed to get away without

Mary tagging along behind him. The last thing I needed was her hanging around.

Tony and his friends weren't there yet. The restaurant was closed on Sundays, just like every other business in Seven Cedars, so I didn't need to help Papa. I could do what I wanted for the afternoon.

I threw the ball right over the piece of cardboard we usually used as home plate. Mike swung the bat and hit the ball so hard it went sailing across the lot. I trailed after it while Mike rounded the bases.

"Hey, Harry!"

I turned around to see that Tony and his friends had finally arrived.

I took off my cap and wiped the sweat from my forehead. "Hey," I said.

Mario kicked Mike's old bat out of the way and dropped a couple of new bats on the ground. He handed a baseball to Jeff Walker, one of Tony's friends, a pretty good pitcher.

Jeff punched the ball into his mitt and spit in the dirt. "So, who's up first? Let's see if either of you guys have what it takes to make the team."

Tony motioned to me. "You're up first, Harry. I know you can pitch okay. But let's see if you can hit."

Mario picked up one of the bats and handed it to me. I tossed my mitt and Mike's baseball onto the ground and took my place at bat. Jeff moved to the pitcher's mound.

I felt sort of shaky trying out for Tony Rossi's team. That's why I missed the first two pitches badly. But I slammed the third one and went racing around the bases. It was a home run.

"Not bad," said Tony. "Okay, Harry. You can play on our team next weekend." He turned to Mike. "Now . . . let's see what you can do. You're up at bat."

Mike had just picked up the bat when I noticed Papa. He was walking quickly across the field. Something had to be wrong. I wasn't supposed to be home for another couple of hours.

When Papa reached us, he put his arm around my shoulder. "Let's go," he commanded. "You need to come home. I'll explain when we get there." He waved at Mike. "You too, Mike."

I grabbed my mitt from the ground. "Sorry," I said to everyone. "See you later."

Mike and I followed Papa.

"Just keep on walking," he said. "I'll answer your questions when we get home."

"What's wrong? Is it Grandmother? Grandfather? Is one of them sick?" I asked.

Papa shook his head, but he didn't explain. He didn't say anything else the rest of the way home, so Mike and I didn't say anything else either.

When we got upstairs to our apartment, the radio was blaring. Grandmother and Grandfather were both sitting

right in front of it. Neither of them looked sick or hurt. But they did seem upset. Grandmother wiped tears from her eyes with a tissue.

"Sit down, both of you," Papa said.

Mike and I plopped down on the couch.

The announcer on the radio said, "We interrupt this program for this special bulletin. Early this morning, the Japanese bombed Pearl Harbor."

"What's Pearl Harbor?" Mike asked.

Papa turned down the sound of the radio. I figured he'd heard this same announcement over and over again, so he didn't need to hear it again. Maybe there'd be more news a little later.

I swallowed hard. "What does this mean?" I asked. "What does this have to do with us?"

"Pearl Harbor is the American Naval Base in Hawaii," Papa said. "The Japanese attacked it from the air this morning. Hundreds, maybe even thousands, of American servicemen were killed."

Mike's face turned pale. "I still don't understand what this means to us."

Papa took his pipe from his pocket. "It means the United States can no longer stay neutral. We're in this war now whether we like it or not. I'm sure President Roosevelt will ask Congress to officially declare war on Japan in the next day or so."

"Will the Japanese attack California?" I gulped. "Will they bomb us next?"

Papa put some tobacco into his pipe, then lit it. "I doubt it. But that's not our biggest problem right now."

Mike and I looked at each other.

"Huh?" I asked. "What do you mean?"

Papa took a puff of his pipe. "Our biggest problem is going to be the way other Americans see us now. To them, we look like the enemy, and they might start treating us that way."

Mike folded his arms across his chest. "That's nothing new. Most people around here already treat us like the enemy."

Papa shook his head. "They may not be very friendly to us. But so far they haven't been a danger. That might change now, though, so we need to be careful."

Grandfather leaned forward. "We protect ourselves."

"That's right," Papa said. "Haruki, you and Mike should stay close to home until we see how people react."

Mike jumped up. "Oh, my gosh. Home. . . . I should be home to see how my folks are doing. They're probably wondering where I am."

"I'll walk you home," Papa said. "Haruki, you stay here with your grandparents. Listen to the radio. There will be more news soon."

Papa opened the front door. A loud crash came from downstairs.

"What was that?" I asked.

Before Papa could stop us, Mike and I ran down the stairs and out to the street. Papa trailed after us.

"Oh, my gosh," I said.

The front window of the restaurant had big, ugly letters scrawled across it in red paint that said, "Japs, go home!" The trash cans from the back alley had been dragged to the front sidewalk. All of the trash was dumped on the ground. One of the trash can lids was still rattling around.

"Haruki, go back upstairs," Papa said. "Mike, let's get you home. We'll take care of this when I get back."

Later that evening, at dinner, I pushed the food around on my plate with my fork.

Papa noticed and said, "Don't worry, Haruki. Everything will be fine."

I looked up at him. "How can you be sure? If Japan bombed Pearl Harbor, won't California be next?"

"I doubt it," Papa said.

Grandfather set his fork on his plate and dabbed his mouth with a napkin. "Bombs not most dangerous thing. People here most dangerous. People not like us now."

"In a few weeks, things will get back to normal," Papa said. "I don't think anyone will harm us."

I felt a lump in my throat. I hoped he was right.

The next morning, Grandmother didn't want me to go to school.

"Too dangerous," she said. "You could be hurt."

"But I can't stop going to school," I said. I gathered my schoolbooks and my notebook from the kitchen counter.

Papa stepped forward. "No, of course not. I'll take you to school. Once you're there, I'm sure your teacher will keep you safe."

Grandmother pursed her lips, shook her head slowly, and left the kitchen.

Papa walked me to school.

When we got there, a few parents were in the classroom, talking to my teacher, Mrs. Gilbertson. I heard a couple of them ask her what she would do to protect us if the school was bombed. I didn't hear what she told them. But some parents took their children with them when they left.

Tony Rossi's mother stopped and glared at Papa and I as she started to leave the classroom. She pointed at Papa and said, "See what you people have done!"

Papa didn't say anything. He stared at the floor. I felt my face grow red, and my fists clenched when Papa didn't say anything back to her. I hated to see him treated that way and just stand there and take it. What was wrong with him? Why wouldn't he stick up for us? We hadn't done anything wrong.

Patsy Simmons, one of my classmates who sat next to me, came into the room with her mother. After they talked with Mrs. Gilbertson, Patsy's mother hugged Patsy like it was the last time she would ever see her. Then she left the school.

Papa went home and I took my seat next to Patsy.

"It'll be okay," I whispered to her.

She wouldn't look at me.

Later, at recess that day, I stood next to the building alone. Mike had not shown up for class, and I hadn't seen Mary out on the playground with her class, either. I was worried about them. I looked up and there was Tony.

"I just wanted to tell you that you didn't make the team after all. You're an okay player. But after what happened yesterday, we don't want any Japs playing with us." He looked around the playground. "So tell your friend Mike. Got it?"

I nodded. It may seem strange, but I wasn't surprised or disappointed. I was so used to being excluded from things by Tony and his group that I never expected to make his team and become a member of his gang. Anyway, I was more concerned about Mike and Mary than being friends with Tony.

"They stay home. Be safe," Grandmother said when I told her I hadn't seen them at school that day.

But I wasn't so sure about that.

Later that day I found out that the United States had declared war on Japan. But I had no idea what that would mean for my family.

Every afternoon that week I was tempted to go over to Mike's house on my way home from school and find out if he was there. But Papa said I couldn't. Then, finally, at the end of the week, Mike came back to class. I had to wait for morning recess before I could talk to him.

Mrs. Gilbertson rang the bell for recess, and Mike and I hurried outside.

"What happened? Where have you been?" I asked.

Mike hung his head. "They took my father away. My whole family has been worried about him. We've been trying to find out where they took him. But we still don't know where he is."

"Your father? Why would anyone want to take away your father?"

Mike sat down on the ground and leaned against the school building. I sat beside him. "The government took him, FBI agents. Since my father's a fisherman, they figured he must be a spy for Japan and can signal their ships or submarines."

"What? That's crazy. How could they think that?"

Mike shrugged. "They're taking in all of the fishermen and questioning them. Some of them come home, some of them don't."

I didn't know what to say. All I could think about was how I would feel if Papa had been taken away and we didn't know where he was or when he would be coming back home.

❖ ❖ ❖ ❖ ❖

The following week, Mike and I were hanging around at my house after school. Someone knocked at the door. I went to answer it. Two men in suits were standing there.

"We're looking for Jirou Yakamoto," they said, as they flashed some identification badges at me.

"That's my father," I said. "He's not here."

I knew Papa was downstairs at the restaurant, getting ready for the dinner crowd. But I didn't want to say that to these guys. I thought about what had happened to Mike's father.

"We'll wait," the bigger of the two men said. He had a crew cut and it looked like his face would crack if he tried to smile. The other man's hair was slicked back and he had huge, bushy eyebrows and he smelled like Old Spice aftershave. Both men pushed past me and walked into the living room. Mike stood there like his feet were cemented to the floor.

The guy with the bushy eyebrows looked around. "While we're waiting we'll ask you a few questions. We also need to search the premises for any contraband."

"Contraband? What is that?"

"Any other adults here with you?" the crew cut guy asked me.

I shook my head. "No one's here but us."

The guy with the eyebrows took out a piece of paper and asked, "Do you have any of the following on the premises—two-way radios?" He looked at me.

I shook my head.

"Pistols, shotguns, rifles, or any other firearms or weapons?"

I shook my head again. "No, of course not."

"We need to check to make sure," the crew cut guy said. "You mind opening this closet?" He walked over to the coat closet beside the front door. Before I could answer him, he opened it and moved aside the coats and jackets that were hanging there.

The other guy went into the kitchen. I followed him.

"Hey, what are you doing?" I asked. "You can't do this to us."

He opened drawers and searched through everything.

A crash came from the living room. I hurried back in there and found Papa standing inside the front door. Boxes that used to be on the top shelf in the coat closet were now on the floor.

"What's going on here?" Papa asked. "Who are you?" The crew cut guy moved away from the closet and motioned for Papa to sit down on the couch. "Are you Jirou Yakamoto?"

Papa didn't sit down.

"Yes," said Papa. "Who are you?"

"FBI," said the man. "We need to ask you a few questions."

Papa looked at me and said, "Haruki, you and Mike go downstairs."

"No, Papa. I won't go."

Papa ushered us to the front door. "Downstairs. Right now. I'll be down when I finish here."

I was shaking inside. I kept thinking about Mike's father. Mike must have been thinking the same thing. His face was as white as a piece of notebook paper.

Papa gently pushed us outside the door.

Mike pulled on my arm. "You heard what your father said. Let's go."

"But they'll take him away, like your father."

Mike perked up a little. "No, they won't. They didn't ask my father questions. They took him away as soon as they found out who he was. Come on."

I followed Mike down the stairs and into the restaurant. Grandfather was there, and the place was a wreck.

"Did those FBI agents search here, too?" I asked.

Grandfather nodded.

"Then why did they come upstairs looking for Papa? Wasn't he down here with you?"

"No," said Grandfather. He sat down on a stool. He hung his head as if he were ashamed about something. "Your Papa at market getting supplies. When he come back, men gone."

"They're not gone," I said. "They're upstairs talking to Papa and searching our apartment."

"We not have weapons. Nothing worth much money," Grandfather said. "What they search for?"

A scary thought went through my mind. "My baseball!" I said.

I started for the door. Mike laughed nervously. "Relax," he said. "They won't take your baseball. That's not the kind of thing they're after."

I glared at him. "No, it's not what they're after. But what's to stop them if they want it? They can just take the baseball and we can't do a thing about it."

Mike shrugged.

Fortunately, Papa came into the restaurant just then. I hugged him tightly for a few seconds, and then I raced back upstairs to my room. I sighed with relief to find the baseball on the floor in my room, still in the red leather case. Everything else from my dresser drawers was scattered on the floor, too, including my socks and underwear. My bed had been stripped bare and the sheets and bedspread were in a heap on the floor.

A few evenings later, on Christmas Eve, Papa and I went to the Christmas pageant at the Presbyterian Church in Seven Cedars, like we did every year. But Christmas Day wasn't the happy occasion it usually was. We were too worried about the war and what would happen to us to do

much celebrating. Grandmother prepared a special dinner for us and the restaurant was closed for the day. But there were very few presents under our Christmas tree.

For the next several weeks life was fairly normal, though. No one came to search our house again or ask Papa any more questions. No one wrote hateful messages on the windows of the restaurant, either. Everyone at school went back to ignoring me the way they usually did. But some of my grandparents' Japanese friends who lived in other parts of the West Coast let us know that not all Japanese Americans had been so lucky.

Japanese Americans in some of the larger cities on the coast were being treated much worse than we were. Grandfather's friends wrote him about beatings and attacks against Japanese-American businesses. I'm not sure how much of what they wrote was actually true. We didn't hear anything about it on the radio. But I overheard people who came into the restaurant talking to Mr. Mack about the possibility of Japanese Americans like us who lived along the coast being sent to special centers in the mountains or in other areas away from the ocean. Some people even suggested that this would be for our own good. We'd be safer that way. No one could attack or beat us if we were in one of these special places. So, in a way, they didn't sound so bad.

chapter four

Leaving My Home

hen I got to the restaurant one afternoon after school in February, Papa was talking to my grandparents about something called Executive Order 9066. This order had been issued and signed by President Roosevelt.

"What does the order mean?" I asked Papa.

"It means anyone living on the West Coast must move inland if the government tells them to," he said. "Right now, we're living in what the government has determined to be a restricted military zone. We need to leave. People who have nowhere inland to go will be sent to special centers to live."

"You mean *anyone* might be made to move, not just Japanese Americans?" I asked.

Papa nodded. "According to this order, it looks like that. But we'll just have to see what happens."

"Why would just the Japanese Americans be forced to move?" I asked Papa. "I realize the United States is at war with Japan now. But we're at war with other countries, too. Yet I'll bet none of the American people who immigrated from those countries will be forced to leave their homes."

Papa seemed to consider this for a moment. "I guess that's because none of those other countries attacked United States soil," Papa said. "Japan did that when its planes bombed Pearl Harbor. If Italy had sent planes over to bomb the United States, maybe Italian Americans would be going to these camps, too."

Tony Rossi's face flashed across my mind. It would serve his family right to be made to move to one of these camps. Too bad it wasn't Italy that had attacked Pearl Harbor instead of Japan.

"We also look different," I said to Papa. "We look like the enemy."

I wondered where we would go. We didn't have any relatives who lived inland to stay with. Most of the other Japanese-American families that my family was friends with lived along the coast. They would be moving, too.

Over the next several weeks, Papa heard from Japanese-American friends who lived in Los Angeles, which wasn't very far from Seven Cedars. They were voluntarily moving to a place called a reception center. From there, they would be sent to relocation centers. They didn't know how long they'd have to stay at these places. Papa's friends told him

we should be prepared to evacuate, too. It was only a matter of time before all Japanese Americans along the West Coast would be forced to move. If we moved voluntarily, we could probably stay together as a family. If we waited, we might be separated. Being separated from Papa and my grandparents was much too scary to even think about.

I was folding napkins in the restaurant one afternoon when Papa came in reading a piece of paper. He told my grandparents and me to sit down so he could talk to us.

"These are our instructions for relocating," he said. "We are going to move to a place called a reception center."

My grandparents didn't say anything. "When do we have to go?" I asked. "And where is this reception center?"

"Very soon," Papa said. "Next month. The reception center is inland, in a place called Manzanar."

"Manzanar? That's a strange-sounding name. Next month? But that's only a few weeks away," I said. I looked around at the restaurant. "What about this place? Who will run the restaurant?"

Grandfather spoke up. "No more restaurant. We sell."

I chuckled. "You've got to be joking. You wouldn't sell this place in a million years."

Papa's face was stern. "He's not joking, Haruki," he said. "We have no idea how long we'll be away from here. We'll have to sell everything—not just the restaurant, but all our furniture upstairs, too. This letter says we can only take what we can carry with us."

I thought about all of my favorite belongings.

"But what about my bicycle? And my comic books, my fishing gear, and my other good stuff?"

"We'll have to sell all that," Papa said. "But you can keep the money. When we come back, you can get another bicycle and new fishing gear."

Hmmm. . . . That didn't sound so bad. I thought about all the money I could make if I sold a bunch of my stuff.

I'd be rich!

I started making a mental list of everything I owned in my closet and dresser drawers that I could sell to build my fortune. But those thoughts lasted only a couple of seconds. I noticed Grandmother's face, and then Grandfather's. They were about to lose everything they had worked so hard for. Papa was, too.

I never thought I would think this, but I felt awful knowing that we were going to lose Charlotte's Place. Although I did not want to inherit it and run it myself someday, I did not want my family to have to sell it—especially to someone who probably would not care for it the way my family did.

And then I had a silly thought. *Would the new owners make everything with love, the way Grandmother did?*

During the next few weeks, junk dealers and other people hoping to buy our belongings for very little money drove through town on a regular basis. Some of them had trucks, while others rode bicycles that pulled carts they could load up with their purchases. They knew Japanese-American families had to sell everything. They took advantage of the situation by offering us much less than what our belongings were worth.

Every time I saw a junk dealer or a white family drive by with a load of furniture, it made my stomach lurch. They were like vultures. Papa sold most of the furniture from our apartment to these people, although we still had our beds so we'd have someplace to sleep at night. Papa said the junk dealers would be back for our beds the morning we left town. I didn't care about the beds. But I had a better idea for selling my personal stuff. I didn't want the junk dealers to get their hands on my favorite things.

I made up a list of items I wanted to sell. I took the list to school. At recess I passed the list around and told everyone to show up at my house on Saturday morning if they wanted to buy anything on the list.

When Saturday morning came, I dragged all my stuff downstairs to the sidewalk. Papa let me use one of the tables from the restaurant and I put a cloth on it so all the things for sale would look really good.

I arranged my comic books in different stacks on the front of the table. Behind them I put my old baseball mitt that I didn't use anymore. I had gotten a new mitt for my last birthday. I had some old building blocks left over from when I was a little kid, and thousands of marbles I'd been collecting for years. I wasn't selling all the marbles. I kept my favorites in a cloth pouch that I would take with me to Manzanar. I also had a cowboy hat I never wore and an assortment of rubber balls, toy cars, and other nifty items. I parked my bicycle next to the table, and I stuck a sign on the bike that said, "For Sale, Best Offer." Papa had cleaned out one of our trash cans and I used it to display my baseball bats and a couple of old fishing poles.

Wouldn't you know it? The first kid from school to show up at my sale was Tony Rossi. He walked over to the trash can and picked up one of the bats. "I'll give you a dollar for the whole bunch," he said.

There were at least six bats in that trashcan and any one of them was worth at least a dollar. It was just like Tony to offer me such a low price.

But I knew something he didn't know. The junk dealer had just come by a few minutes earlier, and he was an even bigger jerk than Tony. He'd offered only fifty cents for the whole bunch of bats.

I turned away from Tony and smiled to myself. "Okay, deal," I said.

Tony left looking pretty pleased for getting such a great bargain. But he'd feel differently once word got around about how little the junk dealers were paying for old baseball bats.

Soon Mario and Jeff showed up. I sold them a bunch of my marbles. And, for some reason, Mario just *had* to have that old cowboy hat. I was able to get much more for that than I had expected.

Most of my really good stuff was already sold when Mr. Mack strolled up to the table. He looked at my bicycle, then pulled the sign off. "I'd like to buy this for Gerald," he said. "How's ten dollars sound to you? Is that fair?"

I gulped. Ten dollars? That was a fortune.

"That's more than fair, Mr. Mack," I said. "You sure you want to give me that much? This bike is pretty old."

Mr. Mack pulled some bills from his wallet and handed them to me. "I'm sure," he said.

I took the money from him and stuffed it into my pants pocket. I thanked him and we shook hands heartily. Then Mr. Mack sat down on the bike. He looked funny because the bike was too small for him. "Pleasure doing business with you," he said as he rode off down the street.

I felt a lump in my throat as he rode off. That old bike was my best friend, like Mike was, so it was hard to let it go. But I took a look at the ten-dollar bill Mr. Mack had given me and I felt better. I'd never had a ten-dollar bill in my whole life.

Papa didn't ask me how much money I had made from the sale. I guess he figured that was my business since he'd told me I could keep anything I made. He probably knew the sale had been successful since most of my stuff was gone and I was whistling a happy tune.

"Come inside the restaurant for a minute," Papa said to me. "I have some good news to share."

I could not imagine what his good news would be. But I followed him.

"Sit down," Papa said.

Grandmother and Grandfather were there, too.

I sat down beside them at one of the tables where our customers usually ate dinner. "So what's the good news?" I asked.

Grandfather smiled and piped up very excitedly, "We not sell restaurant!"

That was no surprise, but I didn't understand why he sounded so happy. I could look around the place and see that Papa had not sold anything yet. "Don't worry, Grandfather. Papa will sell all this stuff in the next few days."

Papa sat down at the table with us. "No, Haruki. You don't understand. We're not going to sell anything in here. The restaurant will stay open while we're gone."

"Huh?" I asked.

Papa leaned forward. "I had a talk with Mr. Mack. He doesn't want to lose his job, so he said he will keep it running while we're gone. For the past few weeks Gerald has been working with your grandmother, learning how to make some of our most popular dishes. He'll be the cook while we're away."

I scratched my head in disbelief. I still couldn't imagine Gerald as a cook.

"Gerald learn pretty fast," Grandmother said. "He can cook okay."

I thought back to the way Gerald always watched Grandmother and Papa in the kitchen. He'd been correct when he told me he would be a cook someday. I never thought he meant it would happen this quickly, or in our restaurant.

Papa patted Grandmother's hand. "Well, he'll never be the cook you are, Mother. But I'm hoping he'll be good enough to keep customers wanting to eat here while we're gone."

"He cook with love," Grandmother said. "I show him how to do it."

"But who will wash the dishes if Gerald is the cook?" I asked.

Grandfather laughed. "Easy to find a new dishwasher. Mr. Mack have other relatives."

Papa leaned back in his chair. He seemed more relaxed and happy than I had seen him in weeks. "Don't worry

about a thing, Haruki. If all goes well, the restaurant will still be here waiting for us when we come back."

"That's wonderful," I said, although I knew I didn't sound too excited. Part of me was relieved that Papa and my grandparents wouldn't lose Charlotte's Place. But another part of me was a little disappointed because they'd probably still expect me to take over the family business someday.

One morning in March I was getting ready for my last day at school when Papa came into my room.

"I want you to stay home today, Haruki," he said. "I'm not sure it's safe for you at school right now. And we're leaving tomorrow anyway."

It was weird. Normally, I wouldn't mind staying home from school. But now that I couldn't go, and I wouldn't be seeing the place for a while, I wanted to be there.

"Figure out what you can pack to take with you," continued Papa. "Remember, you must get everything in one suitcase because you'll have to carry it yourself."

One suitcase? I could get a lot in one suitcase.

I searched through my closet and found an old suitcase from a trip we had taken to Wyoming a couple of years ago. First, I put in my Joe DiMaggio baseball, then my underwear, socks, shoes, pants, shirts, hats, baseball glove, knife (Barlow, got to have that!), the comic books I didn't sell, my pouch of marbles, and my favorite book, *The*

Black Stallion. I closed the suitcase. I *tried* to close the suitcase. It looked like there was twice as much stuff in there as I could fit.

I took out half of my pants and shirts, and a bunch of my comic books, but it still wouldn't close. Then I took out half of my underwear, most of my socks, three pairs of shoes, two hats, and more comic books.

It almost closed!

Maybe I could take a box of stuff, too. Yeah, I could carry a box and a suitcase!

As it turned out, I was the only one in the family to pack a suitcase. Papa and my grandparents packed all of their stuff in big boxes. The instructions we got for relocating to Manzanar said we had to bring our own bedding and linens for each member of the family. We were also instructed to pack enough knives, forks, spoons, bowls, plates, and cups for all of us. We also packed a few family pictures in frames, a teakettle and teapot, an ashtray, a flashlight, some new towels and washcloths, and small religious items from my grandparents' Shinto shrine. Papa packed the Bible, our chess set, and a checkerboard. He tied some pieces of heavy twine around the boxes and made a handle for each one of them so the boxes were easier to carry.

The junk dealer arrived for our beds early on the morning we were to leave for the reception center. Papa's voice echoed through the rooms as he led the man to the bedrooms. After the junk dealer left with the beds, the apartment was completely empty. That's when the reality of the situation really sank in. We were leaving. We had no idea how long we were going to be away and if we'd ever be able to live here again once we came back to Seven Cedars. We didn't own the apartment. We just rented it. Someone else would probably be living there when we returned. I couldn't imagine living anywhere else. I'd lived there my whole life.

I looked around at my empty bedroom. It felt so strange and lifeless without my bed in it and with no pennants and posters tacked up on the walls. Since Grandmother was no longer preparing bread, cookies, and other baked goods for the restaurant, my room didn't smell the same either. No one could cook and bake like my grandmother, least of all Gerald.

Papa walked into the room, his footsteps clunking loudly on the hardwood floors. "I wonder who will live here now," I said.

"I don't know," he said. "But I'm sure they'll take good care of the place, just like Mr. Mack will take good care of the restaurant."

"I hope so," I said.

"Grab your suitcase," Papa said. "It's time to go."

Grandmother and Grandfather were in the living room. They were both wearing coats even though it wasn't very

cold outside. Next to them were the cardboard boxes tied together with string.

Grandmother pasted a huge red sticker on my suitcase. "You know suitcase yours this way," she said.

She had put a huge red sticker on each of the boxes, too. She handed me a jacket. "Put on. Might be cold at new place. Don't know."

chapter five

Manzanar

We had to report to Seven Cedars High School. From there, a bus would take us to the reception center at Manzanar, which my father said was over two hundred miles east of our town. We would be among the first people to arrive there. I hoped and prayed that I would never be separated from Papa or my grandparents. But I was still worried about that possibility.

At the high school Papa filled out some papers, then someone put a little tag on my suitcase and our boxes. They also put a tag on my shirt. I noticed that Papa, Grandmother, and Grandfather also had tags.

We're labeled just like pieces of luggage.

"Leave your belongings here," said a tall, red-haired woman who seemed to be in charge. She told us our luggage would be searched for contraband, then sent ahead

to Manzanar by separate trucks. Everything we owned would be waiting for us when we arrived.

There was that silly word again: *contraband.*

Yes, my family was bringing dangerous items with us to this camp, all right. I stared at this lady and wondered if she realized how ridiculous her statement was. Everything we now owned that wasn't part of the restaurant was in that suitcase and the cardboard boxes.

I opened my suitcase and took out the Joe DiMaggio baseball. I decided to leave the knife in there, though. It probably would be confiscated when they searched my bag. It was the kind of contraband they'd be looking for. But I didn't care. In fact, I felt sort of proud that someone might think I, Harry Yakamoto, a twelve-year-old boy from Seven Cedars, California, was dangerous. That seemed really funny.

I couldn't risk having someone take my baseball when they searched my bag, though. I carefully put it in my jacket pocket.

More people arrived at the high school. I did not recognize them because they came from other towns. Most of them were older people like my grandparents and my father. There were also a few kids, but they were much younger than I was. There were not enough Japanese Americans living in Seven Cedars to fill an entire bus, so our town must have been the pick-up point for several towns in our surrounding area.

We were standing in line, waiting to get on the bus, when Mike, his mother, and Mary arrived. I dropped out of line and ran over to them.

"Your family volunteered to come to Manzanar, too?" I asked.

He smiled. "Are you kidding? We're a team, you and I. No one can break up this team."

We shook hands and I felt relief wash over me.

"Actually, your father talked to my mother about it. He convinced her that it was probably a good idea to volunteer for this, so here we are," Mike said.

Mary grabbed my hands. "Hi, Harry." She gave me a dopey smile.

I pulled away from her, even though secretly I was glad she was here, too. "I'd better get back in line with Papa," I said to Mike. "I'll see you on the bus."

Just before we boarded the bus, a man passed out small cardboard boxes to everyone. I opened a corner of the box and took a peek. Lunch! Inside were a couple of sandwiches (smelled like bologna), carrot sticks, an apple, and four chocolate chip cookies. But the cookies were nothing like the chocolate chip cookies Grandmother made for our restaurant. Hers were twice the size of these and loaded with chocolate chips and chopped pecans. Her cookies were crispy on the outside yet soft and chewy on the inside. There were only about two chocolate chips in each of these cookies. I didn't see any chopped pecans. I would bet these cookies wouldn't be soft and chewy on the inside. They looked like hard, round rocks.

Papa started up the stairs to the bus and I followed him. Inside it was darker than I had expected because shades were pulled down over the windows. Papa stopped in the middle of the bus, stepped aside, and motioned for me to take a seat by the window. I did, and he sat down in the aisle seat next to me. I started to raise the shade on my window, but the man seated behind me reached over the seat and tapped me on the shoulder. I turned to face him.

"Leave the shades down," he said. "It's for our own protection."

At first I didn't understand what he meant. Then I got it. If people noticed a bus filled with Japanese Americans, they might get angry and do something bad, like throw rocks at the bus or block the road.

I left the shade drawn.

Mike, his mother, and Mary finally got on the bus. Mary reached across the seat and brushed my hair as she passed by. Papa grinned at me and raised his eyebrows. I tried to look disgusted so he wouldn't think I was sweet on Mary. She was the one with the crush, not me.

A few minutes later the bus took off, even though there were still some empty seats. We drove about thirty minutes or so and stopped at another loading point. More people got on the bus. We did this a couple of times until the bus was full.

After a few hours, when my stomach started to rumble, I opened my boxed lunch and unwrapped one of the sandwiches. It was bologna. Soon I heard lunch boxes opening throughout the bus and the smell of bologna filled the air. I scarfed down both sandwiches along with the carrot sticks and a couple of the cookies, which were hard as rocks. I decided to save the apple for later, in case I got hungry again before we reached Manzanar.

After we'd eaten, Papa pulled a deck of cards from his pocket and set them on his empty lunch box. I didn't feel like playing cards, so he played solitaire, although the cards kept slipping off the box and landing in his lap.

I thought about the comic books in my suitcase and wondered if I should have stashed one in my pocket. But even though many people on the bus had their faces stuck in magazines or books, I didn't feel like reading. I took the baseball out of my pocket and studied it. Maybe someday a boy like me would be treasuring a baseball that had my name on it. I put the baseball back in my jacket pocket as I felt my eyes getting heavy, and I drifted off to sleep.

Later, I woke up because someone was tugging hard on my arm.

"We're almost there," Mike said.

I rubbed my eyes and looked around. Papa had traded seats with Mike. The shades on the windows were up and I could tell it was late afternoon. I gazed out the window.

The sun was out, but it was difficult to see much of anything. Everything looked blurry.

"Dust storm," Mike said. "We read about them in our science books. Remember?"

Eventually, the dirt and sand settled down long enough that I saw snowcapped mountains in the distance. Then I spotted some buildings under construction, and row after row of other small black buildings. There were also several huge tents. There were soldiers standing around with guns in their hands.

Manzanar was such a magical-sounding name. But there was nothing magical-looking about this place. It was just plain scary.

Mike pointed out the window. "Check out those guns," he said. "They even have bayonets on the end of them."

The bus stopped just as we got to the group of soldiers. Suitcases, boxes, and bedrolls were heaped together on the ground. I scanned the baggage for the big red stickers Grandmother had placed on all our baggage, but I didn't see a single box with a huge red sticker. Still, I didn't care about our stuff right now. I didn't want to get off the bus. I wanted to go back to our cozy little apartment over the restaurant, where it always smelled like baking bread and apple pie. Surely, Manzanar was only a bad dream.

Everyone on the bus was silent. They were all staring out the window in disbelief. I studied the faces of all the people on board. There were old men and women like my grandparents; fathers and mothers with young children; and then kids like Mike, Mary, and me. It seemed to me that not a single face looked like a threat to the United States. There was certainly no one on this bus who needed to be guarded by soldiers with guns.

I felt a lump in my throat. *Why were we being treated like prisoners when we had committed no crimes?*

As people started down the aisle, Mike pulled on my arm. "Come on. Let's see what this place is all about."

I swallowed hard, then followed Mike off the bus.

Papa was already searching through the luggage. Grandfather was helping him, so I went to stand with Grandmother. Mike found his mother and Mary. People around us were chattering to each other. Children played silly games, stirring up even more dirt and dust. Babies were crying. Someone shouted, "If you just got off the bus, form a line here."

I got in line and Papa joined me. He had located our stuff. Grandfather and Grandmother had their boxes. Papa pulled some papers from his pocket and handed them to the person in charge when we got to the head of the line. We were issued ID cards that told us our barracks number, apartment number, and the hours we were assigned for meals. Then we were taken to another building that was only partially completed, with a tent that had been put up at one corner of it. We stood in a long line outside this building.

"This must be the mess hall," Papa said. He studied his card. "No more eating whenever you want to, Haruki. Now we're all on a schedule."

Papa looked tired. More tired than I had ever seen him. As we stood there waiting, he pointed to the soldiers. "Stay away from the guards. We can't trust them. If they think we're the enemy, then they're our enemies."

I'd never heard Papa talk like that before. He was always cautious, but he never immediately distrusted anyone.

"They aren't necessarily the ones who think we're the enemy, Papa. Most of them are probably just doing their job," I reminded him.

Papa didn't answer.

Grandmother was shivering, even though Grandfather had his arms around her and she was wearing her coat. Papa closed his eyes. It looked like he was praying, but I'd never seen him pray outside of church before.

Finally, we made our way inside the building. I figured out why the military calls their cafeterias mess halls. It's because the food they serve there is one big mess. They even expect you to eat it out of tin dishes called mess kits, which are more like metal trays than real dishes. Most everything they served us that evening came out of a can. Canned meat, canned spinach, and canned fruit, which I think was supposed to be apricots or peaches. It was so soggy it was hard to tell. They must have figured we'd want rice along with all this other stuff since we were Japanese. But the rice was bad and they served it with the canned fruit plopped on top of it.

As we passed through the chow line, Papa poked me in the ribs and tried to smile. "We'll have to teach these people how to cook. This isn't American cooking and it sure isn't Japanese. I don't know what this is."

I stared at the lump of rice drowned in peach juice and longed for some of Grandmother's fried chicken with biscuits and fresh green beans.

Suddenly, I remembered the apple in my pocket. I pulled it out and ate it. That was my entire meal that night. I just couldn't stomach any of that other stuff.

After dinner we went to find the latrines. We didn't have to look too hard. We could smell them before we saw them. There were separate latrines for men and women. I didn't go in the women's latrine, of course, but the men's latrine was disgusting. It was a big room with toilet bowls lined up back-to-back in the middle of the floor and a line of showers behind them. The plumbing was not working properly and most of the toilets were either overflowing or filled to the brim. I decided that the shrubs behind the latrine would be my toilet most of the time from now on.

Next we were directed to a block of barracks that were little more than tar-papered shacks set on concrete footings. Each building had about two feet of open space between the flooring and the ground. The wind whistled through these openings. Each barracks was divided into six units. A unit was an apartment that was twenty by twenty-five feet, with a single window, a lightbulb hanging from the ceiling, and an oil stove for heat. The apartments were separated with partitions, but the partitions did not reach all the way to the ceiling, so there was no real privacy. We had one apartment for my grandparents, Papa, and me. The whole place was not much larger than our small living room back home.

Grandmother looked around the bare room. "This it? This all?"

Papa nodded. "I'm afraid so." He set down his box. "Let's go find out how we can get something to sleep on," he said to me.

I set down my suitcase and followed Papa. He stopped another family and talked to them, then we went to stand in another line. We were issued some army blankets and mattress covers. Since no one mentioned mattresses, I wondered why we were given mattress covers. But I soon found out what to do with them.

"Follow those boys," Papa said.

It was growing dark, but I followed the boys over to a huge heap of straw. One of the boys filled his mattress cover with straw, so I did the same with my cover. By the time I filled the cover with straw and dragged it to our unit, Papa had gotten four steel army cots. He set them up in the center of the small room. Papa and Grandmother were

discussing how to arrange them so we'd have a sleeping area plus a living area. Papa dragged one of the cots to the back corner of the room. "Pull your cot back here, Haruki. Then you can set your mattress on top of it."

Papa dragged the other two cots back to the corner, then he and I went back out to the straw heap to fill the other mattress covers.

Grandfather opened one of the boxes, and then Grandmother pulled some bedsheets out of the box and handed a sheet to each of us. I covered my mattress with my sheet and tucked the edges of it underneath. Then I used one of my army blankets as a bedspread.

Grandmother motioned to Papa and said something to him in Japanese. He nodded, then left the barracks. When he returned he had a long piece of rope, a hammer, and some nails. He turned my suitcase up on end so it was taller, then Grandfather kept the suitcase steady while Papa stood on it so he could nail one end of the rope to the wall in front of the cots. He moved the suitcase to the opposite wall and nailed the other end of the rope up there, so the rope stretched out across the room. Grandmother handed him two more sheets and he folded them over the rope, creating a curtain. We now had a bedroom and a separate living area, although there was nothing in the living area but the stove. Papa smiled at the curtain and seemed quite pleased. I knew he was just trying to make the best of the situation.

"We'll find other furniture later," he said. "But this will give us some privacy at least. We can dress behind the curtain."

Grandmother sat down on her cot and put her head in her hands. I thought she was going to cry, but she just said, "Why we have to live like this? What we do?"

Grandfather sat down and comforted her. "Nothing. We do nothing."

Since the sun had gone down, the room was cold. We were tired from sitting on the bus all day, so we got ready for bed.

Sound traveled easily over the tops of the partitions. I heard babies crying and people talking softly as I burrowed under the covers. We all decided to sleep in our clothes even though we had packed pajamas. Our clothes would be warmer. Grandmother even kept her coat on.

I bundled up in the blanket on my cot. I took the Joe DiMaggio baseball out of my pocket and held it tightly, and listened to the wind bang against our little window. As soon as I warmed up underneath all those covers, I fell sound asleep. I dreamed I was back at home in my old, comfortable bed. I could smell Grandmother's cinnamon rolls baking in the restaurant downstairs. Cinnamon rolls made with love.

chapter six

Covered in Dust

The next morning, the sun came peeking through the smudgy window in our room. I was bundled under even more layers of blankets that Papa must have piled on top of me. But I could tell the room was awfully cold. My mouth tasted gritty. I pulled the covers back just enough to look around. My grandparents and Papa were not in their beds. That wasn't surprising since they always woke up earlier than me back home.

A couple of kids were running around in the apartment next to ours. Their feet clopped on the wooden floors. A baby in one of the other apartments was crying again and its mother tried to soothe it.

I forced myself to climb out from under the warm covers. I wiped a layer of sandy dirt from my face with the back of my hand. My bed was covered with a layer of this dirt, too. In fact, the whole room was dusted with a mixture of dirt and sand, white as flour.

Papa opened the door from outside and stepped into the room. "Good. You're awake. It's almost time for breakfast. We need to get in line."

My stomach rumbled, but I hated to think about what breakfast would be like. They certainly wouldn't be serving Grandmother's cinnamon rolls that I'd been dreaming about or the delicious pancakes with hot syrup that she prepared for me on winter mornings back home.

"Come out into the sunshine," Papa said. "It's a bit warmer out here."

I shook the dust from the blankets, folded them, and set them on the bed. I tucked the baseball in between some old clothes in the bottom of my suitcase and put the suitcase under my bed.

"Don't tell anyone about my baseball," I said to Papa. "If no one knows about it, then they won't try to steal it."

Papa rolled his eyes. "I doubt if many people would be interested in stealing that baseball. They have more important things to think about right now. Let's go eat."

I followed him outside. My grandparents were already in line for breakfast.

It was a little warmer directly in front of our barracks because the building shielded us from the wind. Papa and I stood there for a few minutes and warmed ourselves in the sun. But when we got in line for breakfast, the wind whipped right through us. We must have stood there for at least thirty minutes until we made it to the front of the line. I didn't see Mike and his family. Maybe they had decided it wasn't worth it to stand in the bone-chilling cold for food they probably wouldn't be able to eat anyway.

We filed through the chow line and a ladleful of gray goop was plopped into a bowl and handed to each of us. I think it was supposed to be oatmeal. Back home, Grandmother always served oatmeal with raisins, brown sugar, and cinnamon. This was just a sticky gray lump in a bowl. I found a pitcher of milk on one of the tables and poured a little over my oatmeal. The mess hall tent was so cold that I decided to take my oatmeal back to our apartment. Grandmother went with me. We huddled around the oil stove as we forced down our breakfast.

"So cold," Grandmother said. She wrapped up in one more of her army blankets. We were both still wearing our winter coats. She shivered. "Your papa must make it warm in here."

When Papa came back from the mess hall, he examined the gaps between the floorboards and the knotholes in the walls. The curtain had been pushed back against the wall so warm air could circulate.

"That little stove is putting out heat. But there's just too much cold air coming in from all these holes to keep this place warm," he said. "We need to find something to fill in these spaces to keep out the cold air."

"Like what?" I asked.

"I don't know," Papa said. "But we'll find something. Come on."

I set my oatmeal aside and followed Papa around the camp. There were rows of barracks that were only partially completed, and small pieces of wood littered the ground. I found a wheelbarrow and filled it with wood scraps, then Papa and I went through the big trash barrels behind the mess hall, too. We collected all sorts of stuff—lids from tin cans, old newspapers, and pieces of cardboard. We brought everything back to our apartment. Papa took the hammer and pounded the tin can lids directly into the knotholes. He didn't even need nails. The wood was so soft that the tin can lids sunk right into the planks. We stuffed newspaper and small pieces of wood into the holes in the floor. Almost immediately, the room was warmer, but it sure wasn't very pretty.

This must be how poor people live, I thought.

But my family wasn't poor. Papa and my grandparents worked very hard to make a good living. So why did we need to live in a room stuffed with newspapers? It didn't make any sense to me.

That afternoon, Grandfather and Papa found a few larger wood scraps and made a shelf underneath the window. Grandmother removed a couple of framed photographs from her box. She put them up on the shelf as soon as Papa finished building it and Papa added a photograph of my mother that he had packed. He used to keep this photograph of her on his chest of drawers. The photographs weren't much, but they made the room feel a little more like our own place, even though we knew they'd soon be covered with dust.

Grandmother took out some of the objects she brought from her little Shinto shrine. She and Grandfather kneeled on the floor before it with their eyes closed. Papa and I stood there silently. Papa closed his eyes. Maybe he was praying, too.

Not a bad idea. I closed my eyes and prayed for God to get us out of this place.

But, when I opened my eyes, we were still there.

We kept our clothes in the suitcase and boxes so they would not get covered with dust. We didn't have anywhere else to put them anyway.

Even though the room was much warmer now, I didn't want to be there. I figured there had to be something more exciting to do in this place than sit and stare at a couple of sheets hanging from a rope. I went to look for Mike.

It didn't take long to find him. He, his mother, and Mary had been assigned to our block, but their apartment was at the opposite end of the barracks. Mike and Mary were throwing a baseball back and forth to each other. They both had their baseball mitts.

"Hey, Mike," I called out to him, "let's go see what's going on in this place."

Mike handed his baseball mitt to Mary. "Here, Squirt. Take this inside for me. Tell Mom I'll be back later."

"I'll race you to the entrance," I yelled at Mike.

Before Mary could protest too much, or try to tag along with us, we were gone.

After about thirty minutes of trying to find something exciting to do, Mike and I decided that Manzanar had to be the most boring place on Earth. Not only that, but the wind blew *all* the time. It made a high-pitched whistling sound as it echoed across the valley, stirring up dust and dirt as it went. The only good thing about Manzanar so far was that Tony Rossi wasn't there. But it felt strange that every single kid in the place had a Japanese face. There was not a blue-eyed blonde or a redhead in the bunch. Neither Mike nor I had ever seen this many Japanese Americans in our lives. It felt like being at a family reunion where you don't know most of the people. However, you do know you're related to them somehow, even if it is only in a very distant way.

The next day more people came to Manzanar. A huge convoy of trucks and cars arrived with a military escort. Mike and I sat near the entrance, where we could see them all filing into the center. There must have been at least a hundred vehicles, all filled with Japanese Americans. They stirred up so much dirt and sand, after a while we could hardly see anything. By the time all the people had piled out of their cars, they were covered with a layer of pale dust and sand. They looked like ghosts carrying suitcases and boxes as they walked toward us. They had parked their cars and trucks together in a section of the center away from the barracks and other buildings. It made better sense for many people to bring their car or truck with them rather than have to sell it for almost nothing or leave it with a friend for safekeeping. But I hated to think what these vehicles would look like after they'd sat for a while in the sandy wind. Most likely, the paint would be worn off in several spots on all the vehicles within a few weeks.

Mike and I pulled the collars of our jackets up over our faces to shield us from the dirt and sand. We sat there watching the looks of bewilderment and shock on people's faces as they were told to line up to get their barracks assignment and ID cards. We knew what they were all thinking. Manzanar was a prison even though there weren't bars on the windows of the buildings or a fence around the place. And those guards weren't here to keep people from harming us. They were here to make sure we didn't leave. But we were in the middle of the desert. The next town was many miles away. Even if a person did escape from Manzanar, he could get caught in a dust storm, lose his way, and wander even farther away from civilization. He might die of thirst and cold and never be found. It just wasn't worth the risk.

Still, a couple of guards were stationed at different points around the barracks and other buildings to make sure people stayed close by. Most of the guards seemed okay. Although a few of them were just plain mean when someone would stop to ask them a question about where to find something. It seemed Papa was right when he said the guards were the enemy and I should stay away from them. I believed him now, or at least I thought I did.

More people arrived at the center every day. Papa and Grandfather had been helping people fix up their apartments. But within a few days, there were plenty of people arriving who had more experience and skill in carpentry and construction than either my father or my grandfather. They were both left with nothing much to do. Most days, the two of them, along with my grandmother, sat in our apartment. Papa found books to read or he and Grandfather played cards or checkers. But I knew he and my grandmother would rather be cooking, and my grandfather would rather be gardening. But there were plenty of cooks in the mess hall, and how could Grandfather garden in a desert?

I was worried about the three of them. Kids can always find someone to play with and have fun. But I soon learned that grown-ups needed work or something that made them feel useful. I'd never seen my father laze around in bed during the day. It was sad to see him spend afternoons on his cot, reading or taking a nap. Grandmother sat on the suitcase, rocking back and forth with her arms folded across her chest, staring out the dirty little window. She refused to use the latrine during the day, if at all possible, because of the lack of privacy. She said it made her feel like an animal to have to use the restroom in front of a room full of people. She would put off going until late at night when most people were asleep.

One morning we were told to report right after breakfast to a temporary hospital that had been set up in one of the barracks. Mike and I raced ahead of everyone else. When we got there, people were lined up. We both gulped as we noticed a nurse shooting some guy in the arm with a little gun.

"Shots! Why do we need shots?" Mike asked out loud, to no one in particular.

"It's for typhoid and other serious diseases," said the man in line in front of us. "With so many people living in tight quarters like this, contagious diseases can spread like wildfire. Can't let that happen."

Mike's face paled. The man looked at him. "Buck up, son. There's no way around it. You have to get the shots sooner or later. Might as well get them over with now."

Mike and I didn't have to wait in line long for our turn. A couple of nurses went through the long line giving shots to everyone.

They were finished with us in a matter of minutes.

"That wasn't so bad," I said to Mike.

But, as it turned out, the shots weren't the worst part.

The worst part was the stomach cramps and diarrhea that followed later that evening.

Almost all the kids and some of the adults had stomach problems as a result of the shots. The latrines were crowded and the lines were long. Some people couldn't wait for their turn in line. They crouched behind sagebrush and rocks. And I wasn't the only boy squatting behind the shrubs outside the latrine.

We were sick for days, and I spent most of my time in bed or crouched behind the shrubs. I'm sure I lost about ten pounds. Fortunately, Papa and my grandparents felt okay. They had been leaving the apartment every morning and staying away most of the time while I'd been sick. They couldn't stand to be around me when I moaned with stomach pains and they couldn't do anything to help me. Grandmother came in several times each day with a cup of water and a few crackers for me. But I could never take more than a sip of water, and I wasn't able to eat a single cracker. By the time I was feeling better, I had to cinch my belt tighter to keep my pants from falling off.

Finally, one morning I made my way to the mess hall to try to eat breakfast for the first time in a while. When I got there, Papa was in the serving line, dishing up food for everyone. There were hundreds of new people at Manzanar now, so the chow lines were longer than ever.

"What are you doing?" I asked Papa, when I finally made my way to the front of the chow line.

He winked. "I told you we'd need to teach these people to cook. I've taken over the kitchen."

He handed me a bowl of oatmeal. It wasn't a sticky gray blob. It actually looked like the oatmeal we had at home, except there were no raisins in it. I was happy to see Papa so cheerful again.

"How did you get to be the cook?" I asked.

"The other cooks moved to another block. With so many new people here, every block has its own mess hall. Your grandparents and I get to cook for this block now, and eventually, we'll even get paid for doing it."

I looked around and spotted my grandmother filling a large pitcher with milk. My grandfather was opening a can of peaches. They were both smiling. It made me smile, too, to see my family happier now.

I was just finishing my oatmeal when Mike made his way into the mess hall. He must have gotten in line late to wait so long. He sat down next to me and looked at his bowl closely.

"Now this is more like it. We can actually eat the food if your father and grandmother do the cooking."

For the first time in my life, I was actually glad that my father and grandparents ran a restaurant.

After breakfast, Mike went to get his baseball and mitt. I grabbed my mitt, too, and met him out in one of the open fields, called firebreaks, between the barracks. We pitched the baseball back and forth for a while in the fierce wind.

It wasn't long before tagalong Mary showed up with her mitt.

"Can I play?" she asked.

Mike wound up for a fastball. "Here you go, Squirt. See if you can catch this!" He let go of the ball and it went speeding toward Mary.

Surprisingly, Mary caught it.

"Not bad," I said, "for a girl."

Mike wound up for another pitch. He pitched it to me this time and I caught it easily in my glove.

A few other kids came wandering over. Some had baseball gloves, some didn't. The ones who did joined us, and we formed a circle and quickly pitched to everyone in the circle.

"Let's make teams," one of the kids said.

"Yeah," said another. "We've got plenty of kids here. We might be able to form at least two teams and play against each other."

Now that I was feeling better, this sounded like a good idea, except for one thing. We didn't have a baseball bat. Mike had tried to bring a bat from home, but it had been confiscated at the high school before he boarded the bus. Apparently, a bat could be considered a weapon.

"What'll we use for a bat?" I asked the group.

No one said anything. But one of the kids from the crowd stepped forward. He had his hands behind his back and he slowly moved them forward. He was holding a baseball bat.

"Where did you get that?" I asked. "And what's your name?"

The kid smiled. "I'm Ralph. One of the guards gave this to me."

I couldn't believe it. A guard had given him something that was considered a weapon? That was pretty amazing.

"Which guard?" I asked.

Ralph pointed to a group of soldiers talking to one another across the field.

"The younger one," he said. "His name is Private Johnson. He's not so bad. He loves baseball, too. He said we could use one of his bats."

Private Johnson didn't look much older than most of us. And he didn't look very mean. In fact, Tony Rossi looked meaner than this guy did.

I took off my cap and wiped the sweat from my forehead. "Hmm . . . imagine that," I said, still staring at Private Johnson.

Private Johnson looked away from the guy who was talking to him and caught my eye.

I quickly turned away. I didn't want to be too friendly. I still wasn't sure we could trust any of the guards. "Okay, then, Ralph. We need to decide team captains."

I knew one thing. If we were going to form teams, I was going to be captain of one of them. Tony Rossi couldn't stop me now.

"I'll be one captain," I said. "Who wants to be captain of the other team?"

I looked at Mike. "Mike, you want to be the other team captain?"

He shook his head. "Nah. I don't want to play against you, Harry. You're the best!"

I grinned. "Okay, then one of you other guys needs to be captain."

Mary stepped near me. "How about me? I can be captain."

The guys all laughed. "But you're a girl," said one of them. "Wait until they form a girls' team."

"I don't want to play on a girls' team," Mary said. "I'm as good as any of you guys. You afraid to make me captain?"

The guys frowned and shook their heads.

"Go ahead, then. Be captain," I said.

A big, chunky kid stepped forward. His shiny black hair was slicked back, and the sleeves of his shirt were rolled up like I'd seen guys in the movies do. He had a scowl on his face. "I'll be captain of the other team," he said, "not some scrawny girl."

He pushed Mary aside, which made me feel uneasy. He didn't need to do that. He almost knocked her down.

I moved in front of him. "So who are you?" I asked.

He hiked up his pants at the waist, made a horrible hacking sound, and spit on the ground. "Chester Suzuki," he said. "Who are you?"

I punched my mitt. "Harry," I said. "Ever play baseball before, Chester?"

He frowned like I was crazy to ask such a question. "Sure. Back home I'm on a real team."

Chester didn't look like a baseball player to me. Besides being chunky, he moved so slowly that it was hard to imagine him rounding the bases with any speed.

"Good," I said, trying to sound as confident as possible. I should have stood up for Mary right then. Mike should have, too. But we were both too chicken. Chester was a big guy. Mike didn't say anything.

"Then all we need to do now is have some tryouts and then we will pick who we want for our teams," I said, finally.

I looked at Mary. She was glaring at me like I'd just double-crossed her. It made me uncomfortable, so I surveyed the other kids who stood around us. None of them looked like they could play baseball worth a hoot. But I hoped to be pleasantly surprised.

Chester sent Ralph for a broom so we could smooth out the dirt. Another kid went for some boards to use for bases until we could find something better. I heaped up some dirt for a pitcher's mound, and took my place there while Mike called the kids up to bat, one by one.

A couple of hours later I was surprised all right, but not pleasantly. Not a single one of these kids was any good at hitting or pitching, and my grandmother could run faster than most of them. Still, they were all we had to choose from, so we let most of them pass the tryouts.

Mike flipped a coin to see if Chester or I would choose the first player. Chester called heads. The coin turned up tails, so I got to pick first. I picked Mike, of course. Then Chester picked.

To show how sorry the pickings were, Chester chose Mary, even though he didn't really think a girl should play on a boys' team. He even said we shouldn't let any other girls on the team—just her. He commented again about how scrawny Mary was and that she wasn't very fast. But even he couldn't deny that she could catch. She was also a pretty good pitcher, which I'm sure is why Chester picked her for his team.

When it was my turn again, I chose a kid nicknamed Zoom. He was short. But his legs were long for his body and he was skinny, so he looked like a scarecrow. He could run like the wind, but he couldn't hit the broad side of a barn, and he pitched like a girl. Well, like most girls, not like Mary.

Chester picked Ralph next. Then I picked a tall kid named Yoshi. He'd make a good outfielder. Then Chester

picked Arthur, a left-handed batter. But we didn't have enough players for two full teams. We decided to wait and see if any promising prospects arrived at Manzanar within the next few days.

People were pouring into the center on a daily basis. Surely, a few more kids who could play baseball would be among the new arrivals. In the meantime, we'd start practicing with the players we had so far. They could all use as much practice as they could get.

chapter seven

Pitching Lessons

Mike and I were sitting by the front entrance later that afternoon, waiting for the day's busload of people to show up. The wind was blowing as fiercely as ever. But it didn't drown out the sound of pounding hammers and boards being thrown on the ground as workers continued to put up new barracks and other buildings.

A couple of guards approached us. They had rifles with bayonets, as usual.

"What are you two hanging around here for?" one of them asked.

I shrugged. "Just waiting for the next bus to come in," I said.

"Oh, yeah," said the guard. "You two think you can sneak onto that bus once everyone gets off, and leave this place? Is that what you're trying to do?"

I shook my head. That was ridiculous.

"No, sir," I said. "We weren't thinking that. We just want to see if any kids get off the bus who might want to play baseball."

The guard was just about to get in my face when Private Johnson appeared.

"Hey, Stephens," he said to the guard. "They're just kids. Leave them alone."

The guard named Stephens looked at Johnson. "We don't want to waste our time on these little punks anyway," he said, and he and the other guard walked off.

"Thanks," I said to Private Johnson. "We weren't doing anything wrong. We're just waiting to see who gets off the bus today."

Private Johnson smiled. "I know. Well, I need to get to my post. Talk to you later."

He walked off, so Mike and I continued to wait.

Finally, a bus arrived. After a few minutes people started to file out. Mike and I noticed a kid who looked about our age. He was wearing a baseball cap.

Mike poked me in the ribs. "How about him?"

I nodded. But before we could walk over to the kid, Chester pounced on him and snatched him up for his team. Mike and I hadn't even seen Chester waiting for the bus. He appeared out of nowhere, much like someone else I knew back home—Tony Rossi.

Mike and I stood there in the dirt, watching Chester and the new kid walk off together. Chester even had his arm over the kid's shoulder like he was already his new best friend.

"Chester reminds me of someone else," Mike said, holding his cap in his hand and scratching his head. "But I can't figure out who it is."

"Tony Rossi," I said immediately. "Chester is a Japanese Tony Rossi. He appears out of nowhere, so I feel like he's always watching me. Just like Tony."

Mike laughed. "Yeah, that's it! He's another Tony. And it looks like he's found a new friend."

"I wonder if the new friend can play baseball," I said, scanning the crowd for other kids who might make good prospects for our team.

As it turned out, the only other kids who got off the bus that day were girls, toddlers, or babies in their mothers' arms. We decided to go back to practice and wait and see who arrived on the bus the next day.

Mary was already at the field, along with the other kids Chester and I had picked for our teams.

Mary wound up for a fastball and threw it to Zoom.

He raised his glove to catch it, but missed. The ball bounced and rolled into the brush.

"Hey, Squirt," I called to Mary, trying to make peace with her. "You're getting to be a pretty good pitcher."

She grinned slightly. "Thanks."

A few minutes later Chester and the new kid showed up. Chester shoved the kid forward. "This is Dennis. He wants to try out, but I have dibs on him if he's any good."

Dennis was skinny and his hands shook. He pulled on the neck of his shirt, then took off his baseball cap, smoothed back his straight black hair, and smiled at me weakly. One of his front teeth was missing, so he probably was younger than he looked.

I pointed at the bat on the ground. "Okay, Dennis. Let's see what you can do. You're up at bat."

Dennis picked up the bat and got in position.

Mary wound up for a low ball. Dennis swung and hit the ball right back to Mary.

"Out!" she called as the ball landed in her glove.

Mary's next pitch to Dennis was a strike. He missed it by a mile.

But the third pitch was a pretty good hit. He threw down the bat and rounded the bases before one of the kids in the outfield got the ball.

"Good one, Dennis!" Chester yelled. "You're definitely on my team."

When we'd run out of kids to choose from earlier that day, it was Chester's turn to pick next, so technically he had first pick at Dennis.

"Okay, you can have Dennis," I said to Chester, trying not to sound afraid of him. "But let's quit for the day. I'm tired and hungry. Besides, it's almost supper time."

The kids in my block were all scheduled to eat supper at 5:30 P.M. And since our block was full now, it meant we had to stand in the chow line for sometimes thirty to forty minutes before every meal. Most of the kids left to go clean up for supper. I went back to our apartment to drop off my glove and then I headed to the latrine to wash up.

When I finally got to the front of the chow line, I saw Grandmother stirring something in a big metal pot while Grandfather opened a large can of vegetables and dumped them into it. Papa was ladling food onto trays. He frowned when he saw me. "Where have you been all afternoon?"

"Nowhere," I said. "Just out at the firebreak playing baseball."

Grandmother looked up from the pot. "Baseball. Baseball. Always baseball."

I sighed and held out my tray. Papa put some rice onto it, and then Grandfather ladled the soupy vegetables on top of it.

"Tomorrow you're going to school. Then in the afternoon you can start helping out here," Papa said.

"School?" I said.

That was the *only* really good thing about Manzanar so far. There was no school. But Mike and I had wondered when someone would figure out we needed a school and ruin the only good thing this windy sandbox of a prison had going for it.

I moved from the line, sat down, and ate my supper in silence. Manzanar was getting to be a lot like home now. And not in a good "cinnamon rolls and chocolate chip cookies" sort of way. Now I would have to spend most of the day in school, and instead of being able to play baseball every afternoon, I had to help Papa and my grandparents run a mess hall.

I was feeling about as low as I thought I could get when I felt a poke in the back.

Chester.

He didn't say anything. Just poked me in the back to let me know he was watching me.

Yep. Chester was Tony Rossi all over again.

I took a bite of the vegetables and rice.

Ugh!

Even Papa couldn't make soggy canned vegetables and rice taste good.

The next morning, after breakfast, Mike, Mary, and I went to the empty barracks where a few women were setting up long rows of benches. The benches would serve as desks for us for the time being. Other kids of all ages filed into the empty room.

"Good morning," said one of the women. "Come in and join us."

Another woman was sweeping a thick layer of dust into a big pile, while yet another woman put down pieces of newspaper for us to sit on. Piles of clean writing paper were stacked up on one of the benches, along with cans of pencils and crayons, newspapers, some magazines, and a few books.

It was a sorry excuse for a school. But it was all we had, and these ladies seemed determined to make the best of the situation.

Mike, Mary, and I sat down beside each other on the newspaper on the floor and scooted up to the bench. A few minutes later I felt a poke in the back.

Chester.

Sheesh. How could this place be so different yet so much like back home at the same time?

Once it looked like all the kids who were coming this morning had arrived, Mary waved her hand in the air.

"Yes?" said one of the women.

"There's no flag," Mary pointed out. "We always say the Pledge of Allegiance first thing at school back home. We need a flag."

The women looked nervously at each other. I glanced at the can of crayons and piles of clean paper and suggested, "We can draw a flag and use it for the Pledge."

The women smiled and nodded.

Wow! For the first time ever I had done something good at school.

The ladies passed out sheets of paper and a few kids fished through the cans for blue, red, and white crayons.

They didn't find any white crayons, but the paper was white, so we made do with that.

It took us a while for every kid to draw a flag. We didn't have any rulers, so we used books as rulers to make straight lines for the stripes on the flag.

Once all our flag pictures were finished, the teachers stuck them up on the front wall with tacks. Then we stood up to say the Pledge of Allegiance, which seemed a little strange to me now. We were standing in a crummy barracks in a prison, in the middle of the desert, because all of America was afraid of us. And now we were pledging our allegiance to this country's—our country's—flag. Did that make sense? Somehow, it didn't to me. But I let it go and said the Pledge like everyone else.

The rest of the day we did some simple math problems and read some of the old newspapers and answered questions about what we read.

When school was over for the day, I went to get my baseball mitt. Chester had told his team to get to the field by 2:30 P.M. for a special practice. I couldn't let his team get more practice than mine.

Before I grabbed my mitt, I opened my suitcase to take a look at the Joe DiMaggio baseball again and held it for luck. I was doing that when Mike and Mary came by. I'd left the door open, so they sort of peeked in.

Mike noticed the baseball. "We gonna practice with that?" he asked.

I quickly wrapped the ball back up in the clothes and stuffed it into the suitcase. "Of course not," I said. "This is my special baseball."

"That's the ball you won at Weaver's, isn't it?" Mary asked. "You make it sound like it's magic or something just because it's autographed by Joe DiMaggio."

"It's not magic. But it brings me luck. And that's why only a few people, like you two, even know I have it. So don't tell anyone else about it. Okay?"

Mike laughed. "Our team can use all the luck it can get. Sure . . . I'll keep your secret. And Mary will, too. Won't you, Squirt?"

Mary shrugged. "I guess."

I put the ball back, shut the suitcase, and picked up my baseball mitt.

"Race you two to the field!"

When we got to the firebreak, Ralph was already there. He was talking to Private Johnson.

Johnson looked over at me. "Hello again," he said. "You're Harry, right?

I nodded.

"I've been watching your fastball."

I swallowed. How embarrassing. My fastball was my worst pitch.

"Yeah?" I folded my arms across my chest.

"I'm a pitcher for my team in town," he said. "I think I can help you improve your fastball."

Mike and Mary were right behind me. Mike poked me in the back. "Why are you talking to him again?" he whispered. Mike knew that Papa didn't want me talking to the guards. His mother had told him not to talk to them, either.

"I don't think so," I said to Private Johnson. "Thanks anyway."

Johnson put up his hands. "Okay. But if you change your mind, just let me know." He looked at Ralph. "See you guys around."

Johnson turned and walked off. He didn't seem like such a bad guy. Was he really my enemy? It was hard to figure.

Papa was walking toward us now. Papa passed Johnson as he made his way off the field.

"Haruki!" Papa yelled. "What are you doing out here? I told you to come to the mess hall after school."

The other kids stood there with their mouths open. They were about to lose their team captain before practice even started.

"Ah, gee, Papa. I'm the team captain."

Papa grabbed my arm. "Get to the mess hall." He pulled me along with him.

"Mike, you lead the practice," I yelled out across the dusty field.

"Sure, Harry," Mike said.

Grandmother was trying to create a dessert from canned peaches and a few other ingredients. Sugar and flour were both in limited supply, so it would be a miracle if she could create anything delicious. But, if I knew my grandmother, she'd figure out a way to do it.

Grandfather wasn't in the mess hall. Papa said he was out back planning a vegetable garden. I thought about all the vegetables Grandfather grew in his garden back home. The dishes Papa served here at the mess hall would definitely improve once they included foods grown by Grandfather. I helped to clean up the tables and to prepare the mess hall for supper.

That evening, as I was eating supper, Private Johnson came in. Everyone glared at him like he was a spy. *And all because Johnson has a white face*, I thought. In addition, we all knew that the guards and other white personnel were served better food than we were. The evacuees (that's what they called us) resented people like Johnson no matter what kind of a person he might be.

Johnson walked over to my table. "Mind if I sit down for a second?"

I shrugged. I didn't see any way out of this.

"Given any more thought to me teaching you how to pitch?" he asked.

This was the first time any grown-up I knew, other than Mr. Mack, had ever shown an interest in baseball. Back home I would have been thrilled if anyone had offered to help me improve my fastball. But this guy was supposed to be the enemy.

"No, thanks," I said. I kept my head low, hoping Papa wouldn't realize I was actually having a conversation with this guard. I sopped up vegetable juice with a piece of bread and stuck it into my mouth. Papa was still watching us. The look in his eye told me I had better get away from this guard. I got up to leave the table.

Johnson took my arm and nodded toward Papa. "I know your father thinks all the guards are his enemy. And I know some of the guards here are real jerks and make your lives miserable. But I just want you and your family to know that we're not all like that."

He let go of my arm when I looked at him. I thought back to how he'd told those other two guards to leave Mike and me alone. At that moment, I didn't care what Papa thought about Johnson. He was wrong.

"How about a lesson today?" I whispered to him, and he nodded. "Meet me at the ball field later if you want."

I left the mess hall.

It was almost dark by the time Johnson got there, so we just set up a schedule for pitching lessons, then he left. I had one hour after school every afternoon before I had to report to the mess hall. I could devote that hour a couple of times a week to a lesson with Johnson. Papa wouldn't even need to know about it.

After Johnson left, we had a few more kids try out for the teams. James, Goro, and Akio ended up on my team, while Eiji, Ichiro, and Ted became a part of Chester's. Akio said his Uncle George would be glad to be our umpire when we started playing games. That sounded good, and we could not wait to meet him.

The next morning, I went out to the garden area to talk to Grandfather. He was leveling dirt with a rake. "Haruki, look at all this. In a few months we have fresh food and nice flowers. The plants stop dirt from blowing, too. All this good."

I couldn't imagine this desolate plot ever looking like Grandfather's lush garden back home. But the land had been cleaned up and leveled off. I had heard stories from some of the local people who helped out at the center. They said water would be diverted here so crops could be grown. There was also talk of bringing in hogs and chickens to be raised to help feed all the people. It was wonderful to think of us eventually producing food here. But I couldn't imagine this valley without the dusty wind that blew sand and dirt everywhere. Eventually, maybe the greenery would help lessen the sandy dirt blowing all over the place. I thought about pork chops and Grandmother's fried chicken. Mmm . . . I was lost in thought when Grandfather said, "Haruki. You all right?"

I flinched. "I'm fine." I looked at him. "Grandfather, do you think the guards are bad people? Are they the enemy like Papa says?"

Grandfather's hands were dirty and he looked tired. "What you think?"

I shrugged. "I don't know. Maybe they just have a job to do and they have to do it. They don't all seem to think we should be here in this place just because we're Japanese Americans."

Grandfather didn't say anything, so I asked, "So why does Papa say all whites here are our enemies? Isn't he treating them like the American government is treating us? We're the enemy just because we have Japanese faces, so they are our enemies because they have white faces?"

Grandfather pulled a rag from his pocket and wiped his hands. "Your Papa ashamed. He feel angry that people think he enemy because he Japanese. So these white people enemies to him now."

That made sense. But it didn't seem to go along with what we'd learned back home at church.

chapter eight

Plans for a Big Game

It was plain embarrassing to think of us playing an actual baseball game when most of our players couldn't hit or catch. Chester said we should raise the stakes a little. If we didn't, everyone might get lazy and not improve that much. So he made a big announcement that we were going to have our first official game in eight weeks, and he invited everyone in our block to attend.

I shuddered when I heard that. It meant we had only until the middle of summer to turn all these sissies into real baseball players.

We were practicing on the field one morning when a kid I'd never seen before walked up and asked if he could join my team. Mike and I hadn't been at the entrance to the center the previous day, waiting for another bus to show up, so we must have missed this kid's arrival. Mike and I were still short one player for our team, so I was glad this kid was here now.

His name was Andrew and he looked strong and athletic—exactly what we needed to round out our team. We welcomed Andrew, hoping and praying he was a good player. He seemed like an odd kid. He joined Mike and me for lunch that day. All he could talk about as we ate was how great his barracks were. It was the first time I heard anyone say that. The rest of us were always complaining about our sorry accommodations.

"Gee," I finally asked Andrew, "what kind of place did you live in back home?"

Andrew had a puzzled look on his face. Then he grinned and said, "Oh, I had a great place back home. But my family and I came here from Santa Anita. Ever heard of it?"

Mike and I shook our heads. We had heard there were temporary assembly centers and other relocation centers. But we just figured they were all like Manzanar.

"It's an old racetrack," Andrew said. "The barns were converted into barracks, so our room was just an old horse stall they cleaned out. But it still smelled like manure and horseflesh no matter how much we scrubbed it with soap or repainted it."

"Phew!" Mike said. "That's awful. And we thought our rooms were bad. They may be full of dirt and sand all the time, but at least they don't smell like horses or manure."

Manzanar was a lot better than those temporary places where other Japanese Americans had been forced to stay. Papa was smart to volunteer to come here when it first opened. At least we didn't have to stay in a horse stall for several months.

Andrew said the wind and the dust here didn't bother him at all. But as it got closer to summer, the heat began to take its toll on all of us. The camp got dirtier and dirtier as the sun zapped all the moisture from the ground and the daily dust storms grew fiercer than ever. Finally, someone passed out goggles to the people who had outside jobs. They couldn't get their work done without them.

When a busload of new people arrived at Manzanar, it was more fun than ever to see the reactions on their faces. They got off the bus and saw everyone walking around in goggles. Mike and I were sure they felt like they had been transported to the moon or another planet.

To keep some of the dust down, people would turn on a big water hose every day and spray down the soil. This kept the dust down a little and cooled things off a bit. But nothing seemed to help very much. Manzanar dust was always in everything—our clothes, our shoes, our hair, even our food and drink. Our barracks didn't cool down much at night either. We usually pulled our cots outside and slept under the stars where we could get some air. During the day, people tried everything to stay cool. As the days grew longer and hotter, we started playing baseball after supper when the sun had set a little. That was fine with me. It meant I got my chores in the mess hall out of the way before I went to practice, which was great.

One evening after supper I was feeling kind of low. I was tired of not having anything good to eat. I was tired of burning up or freezing all the time. I was tired of the wind and the sand. I wanted to go home. I wanted to sleep in a real bed, in my old room. But I couldn't do anything about those things. Still, there was one thing I could do that always cheered me up. I could look at Joe DiMaggio's signature on the baseball. I'd be late for practice. But I didn't care. I headed for our apartment.

"Hey, Harry!"

I turned around. It was Private Johnson.

He'd been teaching me to pitch for several weeks now. And I'd been right about him. He was a nice guy. He told me he didn't believe any of us should be in these camps. But it was his job to see that we stayed here, so that's what he had to do.

He caught up with me. "Your fastball is getting really good now."

"Thanks," I said.

"Doesn't surprise me, though. You have a real talent for baseball."

That cheered me up a little. "I'm calling it the Yakamoto Fastball."

One day it would be my claim to baseball fame. I could already picture my autograph on a baseball: Harry Yakamoto. I'd write it in big, swirly letters, just like Joe DiMaggio did.

"Where are you going?" Johnson asked. "Don't you have practice tonight?"

I looked at Johnson's honest face. "Yeah, I do have practice." I hesitated for a few seconds, but then I said, "But, come on, I want to show you something first."

Johnson followed me to our apartment. Grandmother had fixed it up. She ordered curtains from the Sears and Roebuck catalog (with money she had finally been paid for working in the mess hall) now that we could receive mail and other deliveries to the center. A friend of hers who worked in the new cabinet shop at Manzanar had made us a chest of drawers. Grandmother topped it with a lacy doily and her small Shinto altar that looked like a little wardrobe with doors on it. But the room was still pretty bare. Nothing like our apartment back home.

Johnson cringed when we walked into the room. "I just can't get used to this," he said. "Making a whole family live in one little room." He shook his head and frowned.

"It's not so bad. We're used to it now. Besides, we don't spend that much time in here anyway. We're always working, going to school, or playing baseball."

Johnson took off his hat and his blonde hair stuck up in the back. "So what did you want to show me?"

I pulled back the curtain made of sheets to get to my bed so I could pull my suitcase out from under it. I opened the suitcase and reached for the baseball that was wrapped inside my old clothes.

"This," I said, as I uncovered the baseball. I handed it to Johnson.

His blue eyes sparkled. "Wow! Where'd you get this? Is this really DiMaggio's signature?"

I nodded. "Sure is. I won this in a big contest back home. What do you think?"

Johnson studied the baseball. "This is great."

"I hold it sometimes for luck or just to feel better."

He gave me the ball back, and I rewrapped it in the clothes and put it in the suitcase.

"Thanks for showing me the baseball," said Private Johnson.

"Sure," I said. "Now, I need to get to practice."

By summertime our meals had gotten somewhat better. Grandfather and many of the other gardeners had plenty of vegetables ready for harvest on a daily basis. There were thousands of people at Manzanar now. It had become a real town in the middle of the desert. We had a post office, a newspaper, and a community store, and our school was no longer just an empty room in one of the barracks. We had actual classrooms with tables and chairs for everyone. We also had real textbooks and trained teachers who worked for the government. They were called civil service workers. My teacher's name was Mrs. Turner. She lived in a nearby town and would drive to Manzanar to teach our class every morning. Most of the teachers lived in town and drove to the camp every morning.

There were no rules that said you had to eat at the mess hall for your block. You could eat at any of the mess halls. So most evenings people from other blocks lined up outside our mess hall because they had heard our food was the best.

One particular evening, Papa made spaghetti and tomato sauce. Grandmother prepared fresh bread and a salad made from vegetables from Grandfather's garden. When I got to the mess hall after school that day, people were already lined up outside. There must have been a hundred people in line by 5:15. Papa whistled happily as he stirred the big pot of spaghetti sauce. Grandmother hummed a happy tune as she slathered more pieces of bread with a paste made of cooked garlic and oil. She put the pieces of bread on a cookie sheet to place in the oven so the bread would get nice and toasty. The whole place smelled like an Italian restaurant.

Mr. Muraki, a cook from another block, marched in with a spatula in his hand. Mr. Muraki was much older than Papa. He had big, bushy eyebrows and thin lips and he was very short. He also had a strange little beard, right in the middle of his chin.

"Where is your father?" he asked.

I was busy tossing a salad that Grandmother had made in a huge bowl. Papa had gone out to the garden with Grandfather to get more tomatoes.

I didn't like the look on Mr. Muraki's face, or the way he waved that spatula around.

"What's the matter, Mr. Muraki?"

Mr. Muraki shoved the spatula in my face. "Have you looked at that crowd outside? The line is a mile long. And most of those people are from *my* block!"

I tried to look surprised and upset, but actually, I felt like smiling. I knew Papa was proud that people preferred his cooking to those of other mess hall cooks like Mr. Muraki. "I'm so sorry, Mr. Muraki."

"It's not fair!" Mr. Muraki raved. "I'm not a professional cook like your father. I just do the best I can. But do people appreciate me? No. They don't. They sneak over to this block to eat. Now, how can I compete with that?"

I didn't know how to answer that question. Luckily, Papa came in the back door just then. He set some tomatoes on the counter, wiped his hands with his apron, and walked over to Mr. Muraki.

"Ah . . . Muraki," Papa said. "How nice to see you. What can I help you with?"

Mr. Muraki waved the spatula around more fiercely than ever and starting speaking in Japanese. I had no idea what he said, but it didn't sound good. Papa stood there

listening. Finally, he asked, "Would you like some spaghetti and tomato sauce, Mr. Muraki?"

Mr. Muraki stopped waving the spatula around. He stood very still.

Papa got a bowl and put some spaghetti in it, then he ladled tomato sauce all over it. Papa offered the bowl to Mr. Muraki. He took a long whiff of the bowl before he snatched it and walked out of the mess hall without saying another word.

Papa and I laughed and laughed.

chapter nine

Papa's Story

news spread quickly in our block, so it didn't surprise me when one morning at breakfast Papa asked me about the baseball team. He sat down beside me at the table while I ate scrambled eggs and toast.

"I figured you'd been playing baseball every evening after supper," Papa said. "And you're captain of a team."

I studied Papa's face carefully. I couldn't tell if he was proud of me or if he was angry.

"Yes, Papa," I said, as I stabbed the eggs with my fork. "I could never get on a real team at home, thanks to Tony Rossi. But here at Manzanar, I can be a team captain."

The muscles in Papa's face visibly relaxed, so I figured he wasn't angry with me. "You can be team captain anywhere," he said. "Not just at Manzanar. You have to stick up for yourself. That's all."

Now I was a little angry. Papa didn't stick up for himself, yet he was telling me I needed to do that. I swallowed a bite of eggs, then nearly shouted at him, "That's easy for you to say. You don't have to face Tony Rossi and his friends at Kramer's Lot every afternoon when we're back home."

Papa wiped his hands on a dishtowel. "No, I don't. But I have had to face men like Tony's father. He didn't want me to succeed with my restaurant or any other business in Seven Cedars, for that matter."

I gulped. Papa had actually stuck up for himself? I'd never seen that happen. I was anxious to hear more.

"So what did you do?" I asked. I didn't want to put Papa on the spot. But if he actually had experiences dealing with bullies, I wanted to hear about them. His advice might help me deal with Chester Suzuki, too.

"I try to avoid conflict whenever I can," Papa said. "But if that's not possible, I stick up for myself. You'd be surprised at how many people stick up for you, too, once you start to stick up for yourself."

Papa pushed up his sleeve and turned his arm out so I could see an ugly scar running along the inside of his right forearm. "This is a little souvenir I got from Tony Rossi's father years ago."

I blinked hard and gulped again. "Whoa! That's pretty nasty-looking. I've never seen that before. How come?"

"I don't flash it around," Papa said. "I'm not proud of it. But once I stood up to Anthony Rossi, Sr., I never had trouble with him again. He stays out of my way."

Papa paused for a couple of seconds before continuing. "Of course, Mr. Mack also stuck up for me the day I got this scar. And I'll always be grateful for that."

I tried to imagine Papa and Mr. Mack standing up to Tony's father. From the long, jagged scar on Papa's forearm, Mr. Rossi must have come after Papa with a knife or a broken bottle.

I wanted to learn more about what had happened that day. I couldn't picture Papa and Mr. Mack getting in a real fight with Mr. Rossi. Not Papa, who always looked at the ground and didn't say a word when people like Tony's mother made mean comments to us. But I also couldn't imagine Tony Rossi, or even Chester Suzuki, backing down from me. Not when Tony had most of the kids in Seven Cedars on his side. They'd do anything he told them to do. And not when Chester was about two feet taller and thirty pounds heavier than I was—the biggest bully at Manzanar. But if Papa and Mr. Mack could make people like Mr. Rossi back down, maybe I could make that happen with people like Tony and Chester, too.

"What happened that day?" I asked.

Papa got up from the table. "Let's just say Mr. Mack and I persuaded Mr. Rossi to stop bothering us. That's all you need to know. Now . . . forget about all that. I need you to concentrate on something else right now."

I took one last bite of my eggs, then pushed my tray forward. "What's that?"

Papa picked up the tray. "A birthday dinner we're preparing for Mrs. Yamagata. She'll be eighty-eight years old in a few weeks. Can you imagine that? Not many people live to be eighty-eight. And most of the ones who do probably don't live in a concentration camp like Manzanar. So we want to have a big celebration and invite everyone in our block to join us."

I was disappointed that Papa would not tell me anything more about his confrontation with Mr. Rossi, but I knew I should drop the subject.

"So what do you want me to do?" I figured he'd want me to bus tables, fill water glasses, or serve birthday cake at the party. The same kinds of things I did back home when someone celebrated a birthday at Charlotte's Place.

Papa stood there with my empty tray. "Help me out in the kitchen the day of the party. Grandmother will be making a small birthday cake for Mrs. Yamagata. And I'm going to prepare Mrs. Yamagata's favorite meal.

"I'd also like you and your friends to make some decorations for the mess hall," Papa continued. "You could do that as a school project. Just ask your teachers. I will also need you to help serve the dinner. I won't have people

standing in line for this event. I want to do it just like we would back home at the restaurant."

I usually enjoyed helping out for birthday dinners back home at Charlotte's Place. So I figured this might be kind of fun, too. I also thought Mary would love it when I asked her to help make decorations for the party. Ever since I let Chester run over her that day to become team captain, Mary no longer had a crush on me. And I have to admit, I was sort of disappointed that I wasn't her idol anymore. Even though Mary tried to be one of the guys most of the time, I knew she enjoyed girly stuff, like making party decorations. I was sure she'd help out.

"Okay," I said. I got up from the table to go to school. I didn't think to ask Papa the exact date and time of the birthday dinner. That turned out to be a big mistake.

chapter ten

One Big Problem

Within a few days, word of the big birthday dinner for Mrs. Yamagata had spread throughout our block. When Chester heard about it, he came charging up to me one evening in the firebreak before we started practicing.

He pushed me in the chest. "What's the matter with you, Yakamoto? Why'd you volunteer to be captain of your team if you're gonna be helping your father with some stupid birthday dinner the day of our first big game?"

I fell back in the dirt. "What are you talking about?" I dusted myself off and stood up again.

"Mrs. Yamagata's eighty-eighth birthday dinner. That's what," Chester said. "Turns out the old lady's birthday is the same day as our first game."

I felt all the blood rush to my feet.

Oh, no! I thought. "Are you sure?"

Chester came toward me like he was going to push me again, so I backed up. "Sure, I'm sure," he said. "I'm not stupid like you are, Yakamoto!"

Mike and Mary came onto the field right then. "What's the matter?" Mike said, as he rushed over to us. Mary stayed back.

"Ah . . . your stupid team captain here won't be playing in the big game with us in a few weeks. He'll be serving birthday cake to some old lady!" Chester said.

Mike looked at me. "What's he talking about?"

"Oh, the party to celebrate Mrs. Yamagata's eighty-eighth birthday. It's the same afternoon as our first big game," I said. Then I thought of something Papa had said about inviting everyone in our block to the dinner.

"Keep your shirt on, Chester! My father is inviting our whole block to this dinner. Everyone will want to come to our game that day, too, so we'll just have to schedule it before or after the dinner. That's all!"

Chester didn't say anything. He just stood there. He was thinking this over.

"Fine!" he said at last. "Then you schedule the game so you can be there! I don't want people saying my team won because you weren't able to play. Got it?"

I nodded and he walked off.

Mary stuck out her tongue at me and followed Chester so they could practice. Mike stayed with me.

"Gee. Chester is so darned sure his team is going to win this game. What a jerk!" Mike said.

"Well, his team is *not* going to win this game. We will not let that happen. I will talk to Papa and try to figure out something."

Later that evening, as we were getting ready for bed, Papa and I dragged our cots outside so we could see the stars. Grandmother and Grandfather usually slept inside. Grandmother would probably come sneaking out to the latrine in a little while, though. If Papa and I slept out here, we could keep an eye on her and make sure she got back to her bed safely.

The wind was blowing as usual, but the ground had been hosed down a few minutes earlier, so the dust would not choke us as we tried to sleep.

"Papa, I need to talk to you about Mrs. Yamagata's birthday dinner," I said.

Papa plopped down on his cot, put his hands under his head, and gazed up at the sky.

"What about it?" he asked.

"It's the same day as our big game," I told him.

"Yeah. So?" he said.

He wasn't making this easy for me.

"So I'm supposed to pitch for my team. But I can't do that if I'm helping you with this dinner."

"Not my problem," Papa said. He bunched up the pillow Grandmother had ordered for him from the catalog, and put it under his head.

Why did he always make it so hard for me to play baseball? Did he really think I'd forget about baseball if I never got to play again? And then I'd take over Charlotte's Place someday? That just wasn't going to happen.

"I know it's not your problem, Papa," I said. "But I don't want it to be my problem, either. That's why I'm asking Johnny Yoshida to take over for me and help you get everything ready for the party. The game will be over by the time the dinner starts, so I'll be there to help serve the food. So, please, Papa, can't Johnny help you that day until the game is over?"

Papa kept staring at the stars. "I guess so," he said finally.

I sighed with relief. "Thanks, Papa. Good night."

I rolled over and went to sleep. I dreamed about pitching at the game and my team was winning. It was the best dream I'd had in months.

❖ ❖ ❖ ❖ ❖

Johnny Yoshida did not play baseball. He wasn't the least bit interested in watching anyone else play, either. So he'd be the perfect person to ask to help Papa with the birthday dinner. Of course, I'd probably have to pay him a huge amount of money to do it. But that was okay. I'd be willing to do that if it meant I could play baseball that day without worrying that Papa would be coming to drag me off the field. I still had the money I had earned from selling all my stuff back home. I could afford to pay Johnny.

I approached him in class the next morning. He wore thick, dark glasses and he always had his nose in a book. Mostly, he liked to read comic books. I thought about the collection I had in the bottom of my suitcase. Maybe I wouldn't have to spend my money after all.

"Hi, Johnny," I said, as I sat down beside him at the table. Usually, I sat at another table with Mike, so Johnny looked at me kind of funny when I sat down next to him.

"Hello," he said. Then he went right back to reading his comic book.

"Can I talk to you for a second?" I asked.

Johnny set down the comic book. "I guess," he said. "What do you want?"

"I need your help," I told him. "As you probably know, I have a big baseball game coming up in a few weeks. But it's the same day as the big birthday celebration for Mrs. Yamagata."

"Oh, yeah, the birthday dinner," Johnny said. His eyes lit up. "I can hardly wait for that. We haven't had cake since we've been here!"

He didn't say a single thing about the baseball game. But that was good.

"Right, the party. Well, that's what I need to talk to you about, Johnny. Could you help my father out the day of the party? He needs someone to set the tables and help with other preparations for the party. I'd do it, but I'll be playing in the game."

I did not want to tell Johnny that there would only be enough cake for Mrs. Yamagata. He would find that out soon enough. Johnny didn't say anything, but I could tell he was thinking about it. I decided to give him a reason for helping me.

"I'll give you my comic book collection if you'll do it," I said.

This idea definitely pleased Johnny. "You've got comic books?"

"Yep," I told him. "And they're yours if you help my father the day of the party."

Johnny thought this over for a few seconds, and then he stuck out his hand. "Deal," he said, and we shook on it.

"Come by the mess hall today after school," I told him. "I'll show you what you'll need to do the afternoon of the party." I got up to go to my regular table. "Oh, and one more thing. You'll need to wear a white shirt and black pants when you serve the food, so you look like a waiter. That's what my father wants. Is that a problem?"

Johnny shook his head.

"Great! Thanks, Johnny."

I moved to my regular table next to Mike.

"What was that all about?" Mike asked.

"I just asked Johnny to take my place helping Papa get ready for the birthday dinner for Mrs. Yamagata. That way, I can play in the game," I said.

"Good idea," Mike said. "I'm glad that's settled."

Chester poked me in the back.

"Me, too," he said to both of us.

My mouth flew open. I didn't even know Chester was in the room.

chapter eleven

The Junior Manzanar Knights

For the next couple of weeks, everyone in our block was focused on two things—the birthday party and the baseball game.

Our school had expanded with all the new kids who had arrived at camp. We had different classes for every grade level now, like we did back home. Mary was two grades behind Mike and me, so she wasn't in our class anymore. But all the teachers had agreed to let their classes make decorations for the birthday party, so everyone was very busy.

One day, as I strolled into class, Mary was there showing a bright orange, short-sleeved shirt with some letters on it to my teacher, Mrs. Turner.

Mary stuffed it into a sack before I could read what the letters said.

"What is that?" I asked Mary.

"Nothing," she said as she closed the sack. "I have to get to class. See ya!"

She hurried out of the room.

Mrs. Turner announced, "Time for class to begin, boys and girls. Please stand for the Pledge of Allegiance."

We had a real flag to say the Pledge to now, so Mrs. Turner had taken down all of our flag drawings. When I went by to get Mike from his apartment for practice one evening, I saw that Mary had tacked her flag up in their window. I threw my flag drawing away. Papa didn't want me to tack it up in our window, and I couldn't blame him. It still felt weird to say the Pledge when our country had us locked away in a camp.

After the Pledge, Mike came into the room in a hurry. Mrs. Turner scolded him for being late. He sat down beside me. I could tell he was anxious to say something to me. But I thought he'd wait until recess. More than once we'd gotten in trouble for talking in class. I didn't want that to happen again. But after a few minutes of squirming in his seat, Mike moved closer to me.

"Guess what, Harry? Chester's team has uniforms," he whispered.

"Uniforms?" I whispered back to him.

"Well, orange shirts with the team name on them, at least. Which is more than we have for our team." Mike looked up at the teacher to see if she was watching us. He didn't want to get in trouble for talking again, either.

So that was what Mary was trying to hide from me in that sack.

"Can't we get shirts, too?" I whispered.

"Chester's uncle got those. He has 'connections,' according to Chester."

Yeah, I'll just bet Chester has connections, I thought.

I put my elbows on the table. Mrs. Turner was talking about something, but I was trying to figure out how we could get team shirts. I didn't hear a word she said.

After a few minutes of concentrating on that problem, I whispered to Mike, "I know how we can get team shirts, too. Leave it to me."

Later that evening, Private Johnson showed up for my pitching lesson. I had pretty much perfected my fastball, so we decided this would be my final lesson. When we had finished the lesson, Private Johnson told me more about the team he played for in his town. As he was telling me about that, I figured it was a perfect opportunity to bring up team shirts.

"Do you have uniforms?" I asked him.

He looked surprised. "Sure, of course we do," he said.

"We don't. Chester's team has shirts. But our team doesn't have anything!" I tried to use my best whiny voice, hoping he would take the hint.

"Gee. That's too bad," Johnson said.

I thought that was all he was going to say, until a few seconds later he added, "I could get you guys some team shirts. What color do you want?"

We had named our team after one of the men's teams at the camp. They were called the Manzanar Knights, so we decided to call ourselves the Junior Manzanar Knights. With a name like that, I thought a dark blue shirt would be perfect. Black shirts would be too hot. But dark blue would be okay.

"How about dark blue?" I asked. "And could you get our team name printed on them?"

Private Johnson nodded. "Okay," he said. "How's silver lettering sound to you?"

"Perfect," I said. "Thanks!"

"Sure," Private Johnson said. "Now . . . catch this!" He wound up for a fastball that nearly knocked me to the ground when I caught it.

The rest of that week I smirked whenever I saw Mary. *Just wait until the game, when she sees our shirts.*

It was just a few more days until the big game and the birthday dinner. Papa was not too happy with Johnny's busboy and kitchen skills so far.

"I'm not sure Johnny will be able to handle this," Papa said one day while we were preparing dinner. "He drops things, and he can't seem to set the table neatly."

I chuckled. "Gee, Papa. It doesn't take any great skill to set a table. But I'll practice with Johnny a few more times before the day of the party. Will that make you feel any better?"

Papa frowned. "Not much. But okay, get him in here to practice," he said.

I ended up having to give Johnny my copy of *The Black Stallion*. This was the only way he would agree to come to the kitchen a few times before the party to practice setting the tables and clearing them off. I'd made the mistake of telling him how many comic books he'd be getting once he finished working at the birthday party. I didn't have any besides those, so I had to quickly think of something else he might want. Luckily for me, it turned out he loved *The Black Stallion* as much as I did. But he didn't have a copy of the book.

Johnny met me in the mess hall one afternoon after school. For practice, he was going to help Papa and me get supper ready for our block. We didn't have tablecloths at the mess hall like we did back home at Charlotte's Place. This should have made things a lot easier for Johnny. All he had to do was scrub off each table after people had finished eating. I told him to get a pail of warm water, put some soap in it, and grab a sponge. But he put so much soap in the water, every time he wiped down a table with the sponge, soap bubbles floated up into the air. We ended up having to get a wet towel to rinse down every table after he'd wiped them with the soapy sponge. To make matters worse, after he finished wiping the tables, he dropped the pail of soapy water. I ended up having to mop the floor and rinse it several times so it wasn't slick with soap residue.

I began to see why Papa was so concerned that Johnny would not be able to handle the birthday party. But it was too late to find someone else. Johnny would have to do. But maybe Johnny wouldn't have to scrub down all the tables. I could do that before the game. *Yeah, that's what I would do!*

chapter twelve

The Big Game

The day of the big game arrived. I made sure Johnny had on a white shirt and black pants, just like Papa wanted. I'd gotten him settled in at the mess hall with Papa, and I'd scrubbed down all the tables. Papa looked at the bare tables and said he wished we had tablecloths. But there wasn't anything I could do about that. I hurried out to start the game.

When I got to the firebreak, all the other players were on the field. And Uncle George, as we all called him now, was behind home plate, ready to umpire. It was time to play. I put on my glove.

Chester's team members were easy to pick out. They looked like large, funny pumpkins in their bright-orange shirts with the name Manzanar Daze printed on the front.

Private Johnson had come through for me. Everyone on my team was decked out in dark blue shirts with Junior Manzanar Knights printed in shiny, silver letters.

Mary threw me the ball.

I stepped onto the pitcher's mound.

Mike was catching.

I threw several pitches to warm up.

Mike dropped a couple of my fastballs. My fastball was really fast now. On the second dropped pitch, Mike picked up the ball and the team threw it around the horn. Mike threw it to Zoom at third base, who threw it to Andrew at shortstop, who threw it to James at second, who threw it back to Zoom at third. Zoom then threw the ball back to me.

Chester's team whistled and hooted.

"Let's get going!" Chester shouted.

"Just a couple more," I said. I wasn't sure I had the best action on my pitches today.

Chester yelled, "Is that your best stuff?"

Oh boy, I thought. *This could be a long day.*

Dennis stepped into the batter's box we had marked with chalk in the dirt. He took a few practice swings, then settled into his stance, wriggling the bat next to his head.

Mike gave me the signal for a fastball.

I shook my head.

Mike signaled for a curveball.

I nodded. I got my best action on a curveball.

The ball curved away from Dennis as he took a big swing and missed, almost making himself turn in a circle.

"Strike one!" yelled the umpire.

My team cheered, clapped, whistled, and stomped the ground.

"Keep it coming!" someone yelled.

Mike gave the signals and I got two more quick strikes. My first strikeout.

"Throw it around the horn," I said.

The next batter was Edward. He was about four feet tall and not much thicker than the bat. Since he was so short, there was no strike zone.

I was nervous. I threw four balls—a walk—allowing Edward a free pass to first base.

Joseph stepped into the batter's box.

Now there was one out and a player on first.

Mike signaled a fastball.

I nodded, wound up, and threw a blistering fastball right over the plate.

"Strike one!" the umpire announced.

Mike signaled for another fastball.

I nodded.

I threw it just as hard this time, but it was outside the plate for ball one.

My next pitch curved sharply away as the batter swung for strike two.

My next fastball and curve ball went for balls.

Now the count was full: three balls and two strikes.

Mike signaled for a fastball. I wound up and threw. The ball didn't have as much juice on it as before—not enough speed and a little too high. The batter made a tremendous uppercut, and "Crack!" went the bat.

The ball sailed way over the outfield. The batter and the runner already on base reached home plate before my team could get the ball back to the infield.

I felt horrible. I had allowed an inside-the-park home run. The score was 2–0 for the Daze—Chester's team.

The next two batters were easy outs. Now it was our turn to bat.

I was up first. Mary was pitching for Chester's team.

The first pitch was outside. Ball one.

Pitch two was right down the middle of the plate for strike one. I wasn't ready for that. I tried to concentrate on the ball and not who was pitching. All I had to do was wait for a good pitch.

Mary threw ball two. Then ball three. Then ball four—a walk. I was on base.

Mike followed me at bat. He hit a home run!

The game was tied, 2–2.

Unfortunately, no one else on my team could hit well. James grounded out to first. Andrew struck out, and Zoom hit a pop-up fly ball that Chester caught with ease. So, just like that, the first inning was over.

Mary tossed me the ball.

Arthur was up next, a left-hander. It was a good chance to try my fastball again. The ball left my hand and flew to the right, away from the left-hander.

"Strike one," the umpire called.

I threw another one.

Arthur reached out but only caught a piece of the ball. It rolled outside the base path. Foul ball.

"Strike two!"

I didn't know if I should try the same pitch three times in a row, so I switched to a curveball. For a lefty, the ball would curve right into him.

I waited for the curveball sign from Mike.

I nodded.

The pitch was kind of wild—way right. It ended up about where my fastball had been, but the kid swung and missed—strike three.

I had thrown three pitches and got three strikes, so I was feeling pretty good.

The next batter was Chester. He popped up for an out. He got angry and slung the bat across the field. That rattled me and I lost some of my stuff. I gave up a walk. The next batter, though, hit it straight to Zoom at third base for the third out.

The game continued like that clear up until the seventh inning. I would pitch pretty well, and then they would get a hit or score. When it was our turn to bat, we would do the same. Mary was a pretty good pitcher—but not quite as good as me. Some innings nobody scored. Three up and three down, as the saying goes.

At the seventh inning stretch, the score was 5–4, in favor of the Junior Manzanar Knights.

Then the unthinkable happened. I looked up from swinging the bat and there was Papa, coming toward the baseball field. I froze. *Oh, no!*

"You've got to help," Papa said. "Johnny is a disaster. I need you, Haruki. Let's go."

My whole team let out a groan. They knew when Papa spoke, I had to obey. It was the Yakamoto way.

At least we had the lead. For now. I walked off the field. I dropped the bat on the ground by our bench.

"Akio," I yelled. "You pitch if we take the field again before I get back. We'll have to get by with eight batters and no center fielder. I'll be back soon, I hope."

I looked at Mary.

"See ya," she said. She didn't look upset one little bit that I was leaving. Yep. Her crush on me was long gone.

I raced to the mess hall with Papa trailing behind me. When we got there, I opened the door and charged in. If Johnny thought he would get even one of my old comic books now he was sadly mistaken.

Mike's mother and a bunch of other ladies were tacking up a big banner on the wall. I think it said "Happy 88th

Birthday, Mrs. Michiko Yamagata!" in Japanese, but I wasn't sure. It stretched out all the way across the room.

Johnny was wrestling with big pieces of white butcher paper.

"What are you doing?" I asked him. I took off my baseball hat and tossed it aside.

Johnny stood up and let go of the paper. "Your father wants the tables covered with this paper," he said. "He says the tables are too plain. And this paper will look almost as good as a tablecloth. But I can't seem to smooth down the pieces the way he wants. The paper keeps bunching up before I can stick it down with these tacks."

"Oh, for gosh sakes," I said. "Let me wash my hands and I'll tack the paper down. You go find out what else Papa needs you to do."

Johnny stood there looking at me like he hadn't heard a word I said.

"Go!" I shouted to him, and finally he took off quickly to find Papa.

After I washed the dirt and grime from playing baseball off my hands, I smoothed down the paper and secured it with the tacks. It wasn't as nice as a tablecloth, but Papa was right, it looked better than just a bare, banged-up, old wooden table. I found the roll of butcher paper standing in a corner. I lugged it with me to another table, cut off a piece of paper a little longer than the length of the table, then stretched it across the table and secured it with some tacks. I did three or four more tables this way. But I couldn't get my mind off the game.

Akio wasn't a good pitcher. But since he played center field, he was the most expendable player on the team. Goro and Yoshi, the right and left outfielders, could take up the slack while Akio pitched. Harold needed to stay in as shortstop and all the other players were needed to cover the bases. It seemed like a good decision when I'd said to put Akio in as pitcher. But now I wasn't so sure about that. I just *had* to get back out to the game, or we were sunk.

I finally got the paper on all the other tables. Johnny would have to do a good job with everything else. I looked around for Papa. When I didn't see him, I dashed out of the mess hall.

I started back to the game, but then I thought of something.

Maybe I should get my Joe DiMaggio baseball. Have it with me, just for luck.

I made my way back to our apartment and pulled the suitcase out from under my bed. I rummaged through it until I found the old clothes that I used to wrap up the baseball.

I found the clothes.

But the baseball wasn't there.

Huh? How could that be?

I dumped everything out of the suitcase onto the floor and combed through every piece of clothing.

Still, no baseball.

I felt as if someone had just cut out my heart. I couldn't breathe.

Someone took my baseball? Who would do such a thing? No one even knew I had it!

But then I realized I was wrong about that.

Papa and my grandparents knew about the baseball.

But Papa wouldn't take my baseball. Would he? He could not be that desperate to have me help out at Mrs. Yamagata's birthday party!

Then I remembered the day I had shown the ball to Private Johnson.

Did he take it for luck? Would he betray me like that, by stealing my most prized possession? Was Papa right about him after all?

My mind was racing in circles.

It had to be Private Johnson. No one else knew about the baseball—no one else but Mike and Mary.

Wait a minute. . . .

I charged out of the room and ran as fast as I could. I got back to the game. The score was 9–6 in favor of the Daze. It had not gone well while I was gone.

"What have you guys been doing?" I asked.

"We did our best. We got one run," Zoom said.

It was the ninth inning. Somehow we had kept them from scoring in the ninth.

Now it was our chance, our last chance—the bottom of the ninth, down three runs. Mary was pitching.

Zoom was up first. Mary was getting tired. She threw four quick balls and Zoom went to first base.

Next up was Andrew. He took three quick strikes. One out now.

James was next. He got a base hit. This put runners on first and second.

Akio followed James and struck out, too.

Mike was next. He had seen this kind of pitching before. He took Mary's curveball and hit it for a single. The bases were loaded.

I was up next.

As I walked up to the plate, I was a little nervous.

"This one is all over, everyone!" Chester shouted. "Yakamoto's at bat. He can't hit under pressure!"

I scowled at Chester . . . *That's what you think.*

Mary wound up and pitched a fastball right down the middle.

"Strike one!"

She was good—very good. I should have been ready for that one.

The next pitch was low. The catcher dropped it. The catcher scooped up the ball and threw it to Mary.

One ball and one strike. Mary was a good pitcher. But I knew every pitch she had. *Could I hit whatever she pitched?*

Mary wound up and threw.

Curveball, I thought. *Not her best pitch.*

"Ball two!"

The catcher threw the ball back to Mary.

She threw a curveball next. A little outside for ball three. I had to watch that one like a hawk. She threw another curveball. I saw it coming, but could only catch the edge of the ball—a foul ball.

So here I was. Three balls and two strikes. Two outs and the bases loaded. One of my best friends pitching, but she was mad at me. Mary wound up. She pitched.

Fastball, I thought. *Her best pitch.*

The ball came in right over the center of the plate. It seemed like slow motion. I poised on my back leg, then stepped onto my front leg.

Crack! The best sound you'll ever hear. The ball sailed way over the outfield.

Zoom tagged home plate.

James tagged home plate next.

Mike was third.

And then me, Harry. The winning run. I raised my arms; I didn't know what else to do.

Our fans went wild. They cheered, clapped, whistled, hooted, hollered, and screamed.

I looked at the crowd. Papa, Grandfather, Grandmother, Mrs. Yamagata . . .

Mrs. Yamagata?

Yep. Eighty-eight-year-old Mrs. Michiko Yamagata! She cheered right along with everyone else. And there was one other face I hadn't expected to see. One other face that everyone, including me for a couple of seconds, thought of as the face of the enemy—Private Johnson.

He whooped and hollered right along with everyone.

After tagging home plate, I went up to Mary on the pitcher's mound.

"Good game," I said.

"Sorry about the special baseball," Mary said. "I guess it really doesn't bring good luck after all."

I reached out for the Joe DiMaggio ball. She dropped it in my hand.

"You're one heck of a hitter, Harry. Good game."

"Thanks, Mary," I said, then I slipped the baseball into my pocket.

chapter thirteen

A Letter From Joe

People were still cheering. Papa picked me up and carried me back to the mess hall on his shoulders. The rest of my team followed us. Chester's team—in their bright pumpkin shirts—slowly trailed behind, too. Chester grumbled at Mary. She didn't look very happy. But I couldn't worry about that now. This was my moment in the spotlight.

When Papa set me down at the mess hall, I gave him a hug. "You came to the game!" I said. "I didn't think you would. But what about the party?"

"Everything is ready for the party. Johnny was here watching things while your grandparents and I watched the rest of the game."

I rolled my eyes. I could not believe Papa had left Johnny in charge of things even for a minute.

"You left Johnny in charge? Wow," I said. Then I glanced at the door. Private Johnson had just walked in.

Uh-oh. I closed my eyes and cringed, thinking of what Papa would say to him. Surely he'd think Johnson would ruin the party.

"Private Johnson!" Papa shouted. "Come in! Come join the party!"

I opened my eyes. *What is going on?*

Private Johnson joined us. He shook my hand so hard I thought it was going to fall off. "Great game there, Harry! Congratulations! That was some fastball of yours! And you're a great hitter, too!"

Papa motioned for Johnny, and Johnny came over. "Show Private Johnson his seat, Johnny," Papa said.

"Right this way, Private Johnson," Johnny said, and the two of them walked off.

I scratched my head. "Papa, what's going on? What is Private Johnson doing here? And why are you being so nice to him?"

Papa pulled me back to the kitchen where we could talk privately.

"When you left to go back to the game a while ago, I went to our apartment searching for you. I figured you would go there to get that baseball for luck. When I got there, you were gone. The baseball was gone, too, so I thought you had it. But I ran into Private Johnson outside the mess hall. He told me he'd seen you racing out of our apartment without the baseball. He knew something bad had happened. Someone had taken it."

I backed up and sat down in a chair.

Papa touched my shoulder. "I was wrong about Private Johnson. He's a good man. He told me he has helped you with your pitching. I'm proud of you, Haruki. You're a good son. You did not let my bitterness about being here at Manzanar rub off on you. You made me see that not all whites hate us. When Private Johnson realized you did not have that special baseball, he said you would need all the support you could get if you were going to win that big game."

I looked up at Papa. "So that's why you, Grandmother, and Grandfather were at the game," I said.

Papa nodded.

I hugged him again. "Johnson is a good man, Papa. And so are you! I love you, Papa."

Papa put his arms around me and hugged me tight. "I love you, too, Haruki. But now . . . we'd better get back out there and get this party started. Don't you think?"

Papa and Grandmother had outdone themselves this time. All the school classes had done a great job with the decorations, too. They had even made streamers and little kazoos for everyone to play. Finally, a small part of Manzanar looked magical. The mess hall was beautiful.

The table of honor was stacked with homemade birthday cards from almost every person who lived in our block. Mrs. Yamagata was escorted to the table and Mike's mother put a party hat on her head. It looked like a crown and she was the queen of Manzanar.

Papa had my white shirt and black pants ready for me to change into. I went to clean up first. Then I put on the clothes so I looked more like a waiter than a baseball player.

A pitcher of fresh flowers from Grandfather's garden was the centerpiece for each table. The butcher paper I'd covered the tables with earlier didn't look half bad once the flowers, dishes, and food were on the tables. Someone had even made Japanese paper lanterns that were strung all across the room.

I helped Papa serve the meal when he told Johnny and me that everything was ready.

"You can clear the tables when people have finished eating," I said to Johnny. "That way it won't matter so much if you drop anything."

He seemed relieved at that suggestion.

After having to stand in line for meals each day, there were whispers about how nice it was to be served at the table again, like back home or in a restaurant. I hoped Papa overheard that. I knew it would make him happy.

Papa had said he would be serving Mrs. Yamagata's favorite dish for this meal: baked trout. But I didn't see how he would pull that off. But sure enough, Papa handed me a plate heaping with rice, steamed vegetables, and baked trout. He told me to take it to Mrs. Yamagata. I took it to her table and set it before her. She swooned with delight, and then her eyes began tearing up. Papa walked over to her table and kissed her on the cheek.

"How did you manage to get fresh trout?" I asked Papa when he was back at the stove, serving up more food for everyone else.

"Grandfather and I did a little fishing," he said.

I'd heard stories about men at Manzanar sneaking out of the camp to do some fishing. But I hadn't believed those stories, until now.

Yet even Papa and Grandfather could not provide enough fish for the whole block, so everyone else was served vegetable *sukiyaki*. Papa made this Japanese dish with vegetables from Grandfather's garden. He knew most of the people at Manzanar would enjoy a real Japanese meal for a change.

Finally, everyone finished eating, and Johnny and I started clearing the tables. As we were taking the dishes from the last table, I heard a drumroll, then some cymbals clashed. Papa wheeled out a cart with a small birthday cake on top of it. The cake was little more than a cupcake. Poor Johnny. He was looking forward to having cake tonight. But that really didn't matter. All that mattered was that Mrs. Yamagata had a wonderful birthday and everyone had fun helping her celebrate.

People sang "Happy Birthday," then Papa made a joke by telling Mrs. Yamagata to blow out the candles. Everyone laughed. We all applauded when she blew out the one tiny candle on the little cake.

After the guests began to leave, Papa told me to eat.

The minute I sat down at a table I felt like I would fall asleep. It had been a long, exciting day. But now I was exhausted. I ate a little of the *sukiyaki*, then I put my head down on the table. People were still laughing and talking as they were leaving, but the noise didn't bother me. I went right to sleep.

Then I felt a poke in the back.

Chester.

I sat up, rubbed my eyes, and yawned. "What is it, Chester? Can't you ever leave me alone?"

"I heard about your magic baseball," he said. "I'm not so sure you won that game fair and square if you used a magic baseball when it was your turn to pitch."

I looked at Chester and grinned.

"I didn't use a magic baseball, Chester. We won the game fair and square all right."

"Oh, yeah?" asked Chester. "Then what's the story about the magic baseball?"

"I won it in a contest back home," I told him. "It's not magic. It's just special. It has Joe DiMaggio's autograph on it."

"Really?" Chester said. "Can I see it?"

I'd left the baseball in the pocket of my other pants when I changed clothes, or I would have shown it to him right then. "Sure, I'll show it to you sometime."

Chester's eyes widened. "Did you get to meet him in person?"

"Who?" I asked, half forgetting who we'd been talking about.

"Joe DiMaggio, you dope."

All of a sudden my head felt funny and my stomach ached. "No, I didn't meet Joe DiMaggio in person. I just got the baseball. That's all. I gotta go now, Chester. See you later."

I got up from the table, went to the back and grabbed my baseball clothes. Then I slipped out of the mess hall before Papa could figure out I was gone. I walked to our apartment and rummaged through my suitcase again. The baseball case was still there, but Mary hadn't rewrapped it in the clothes. I took it out and put the baseball back in it. But before I closed the case, I took out the envelope with the letter of invitation from Joe DiMaggio. I lay down on my cot, opened the letter, and reread it for about the millionth time. If we hadn't been forced to leave home, I would be meeting Joe DiMaggio this very month. It was the chance of a lifetime. A chance that I was now going to miss—forever.

I fell asleep with the letter still clutched in my hands. The next morning, I got up and put the letter back in my suitcase just as Papa opened the door and came into our apartment.

"Haruki, I have something to show you," he said.

By now we had a few chairs in our room, so Papa pulled one over and sat down beside me.

"Is something wrong, Papa?"

"No, nothing's wrong. In fact, I'm hoping to make something right for a change."

I had no idea what Papa was talking about.

"I've always known how important baseball is to you, Haruki. I know I haven't always acted like it. But it's true. And when you won that baseball in the contest I knew how much it meant to you. I also knew how much you were looking forward to meeting Joe DiMaggio."

I hung my head. That was never going to happen now. But that wasn't Papa's fault.

"Anyway," continued Papa. "Once I realized we were going to be at Manzanar for quite a while, I searched for that letter of invitation you won. I wanted to see if it would tell me how to contact Mr. DiMaggio."

My eyes were wide open now. "Why did you want to contact Joe DiMaggio?"

"To tell him how disappointed you would be that you wouldn't get to accept his invitation and meet him this summer."

I gasped. "Oh, Papa. Did you get in touch with him? Did you?"

Papa leaned forward and offered me the envelope he'd been holding.

"I sure did. This is for you."

I tried not to snatch the envelope. My hands were shaking as I opened it and pulled out the paper inside it.

It was a letter from Joe DiMaggio. The first thing I noticed as I read was that he called me Harry, not Haruki. I wondered if Papa had had anything to do with that.

Dear Harry,

I'm so pleased to know that you're my number one fan. Your family has written and told me all about your situation and how you will be unable to visit me this summer in Los Angeles. I'm so sorry about that. War causes people—and entire countries—to do strange things to each other.

Someday soon, when this war is finally over, you'll have to come visit me in New York. I'll send you and your family free tickets to a Yankees game anytime you're available. Then we'll have a special dinner afterward so we can get to know each other.

We all must be brave during these troubled times. And it sounds like you are a very brave young man. Keep playing baseball. Maybe someday you'll pitch for the New York Yankees.

Sincerely,
Joe DiMaggio

I reread the letter several times before placing it back in the envelope.

Then I got up from the cot and hugged Papa. "Thank you, Papa! This letter is even better than the baseball."

There were tears in Papa's eyes. I wasn't sure why. I was also confused about something else.

"Why did he send this letter to you, Papa? Why didn't he mail it directly to me?"

"I wanted to be sure you read this after your first big game," Papa said. "Whether you won or lost that game, I figured the best time for you to read it would be after the game. If you lost the game, reading his letter would cheer you up. But if you won the game, then the letter would make you feel that much happier. Was I right about that?"

I smiled and wiped away the tears that had formed in my eyes.

"Yes, Papa, you were right about that!"

Epilogue

The Best Baseball Player in Seven Cedars

Winning the first real baseball game of my life that day at Manzanar—and realizing I did not need a special baseball for luck in order to do it—taught me a lot about myself and my family.

Papa, my grandparents, and I—and thousands of other Japanese Americans—spent over three years at Manzanar. During that time, more than eighty baseball teams were formed at the camp, including many girls' teams. Mary eventually switched to a girls' team, but she always had the best fastball of any girl (and most boys) in the camp.

Within our first year at Manzanar, a barbed wire fence was constructed around the entire camp, and eight guard towers were built so the guards could keep watch over us at all times. This made the place look and feel like a prison even more than it did the day we arrived. But for the most part, all the evacuees at the camp worked hard to improve their surroundings and make the best of the situation.

Grandfather and his friends were not the only ones gardening within a year or so. Eventually, most of the food we ate was grown at Manzanar, including chicken and pork. They did finally set up those hog and chicken farms. Japanese Americans at Manzanar also helped in the war effort. The camp housed a camouflage-net factory at one point, although it closed after a riot broke out in the camp on December 6, 1942. Two people, including a seventeen-year-old boy, were killed, and many others were injured. But this riot was the only widespread incident of violence that took place during our entire stay at Manzanar.

By March 1945, only a few people remained at the camp. Papa, Grandmother, Grandfather, and I were among them. But it was time for us to go home, too.

A chilly wind whistled through Manzanar as we waited inside the gate for the bus that would take us back home. I noticed how different this place had become over the three years we had lived here. It had been transformed from a dry and dusty, uninhabited spot in the desert into a home for thousands. But I wondered what would become of the place after we all left. Within a few years, would all of this be gone, and no one would even remember what had once been here? Would people look back and learn from all this? I didn't know the answers to those questions. I wondered if anyone did.

I was almost as scared to go back home as I had been to leave. Over the years, Papa had received regular letters from Mr. Mack. We knew that he had closed the restaurant. Although Gerald prepared everything on the menu with love, just like Grandmother had taught him to do, he never did become the great cook Grandmother was. In addition, money was very tight during the war and fewer people were eating out at restaurants. With fewer and fewer customers, Mr. Mack finally had no choice but to close the restaurant. We had nothing to go back home to now—no apartment and no business. Still, Seven Cedars was home. Papa would find work there. I was old enough to get a job after school now. We'd rebuild our lives somehow.

The big, ugly gray bus pulled into camp and honked its noisy horn.

People lined up to board. Mike and I were going to sit together, and we were at the front of the line until Chester pushed ahead of us. "Come on, Mary," he said, pulling her with him.

Ever since Chester had picked Mary for his team three years ago, he treated Mary like she was his property. Mary didn't seem too happy about it. But she didn't mind enough to do anything about it. I kept wondering what she was waiting for.

Then, all of a sudden, I knew.

I yanked Chester by the arm. Something I had never had the courage to do. He let go of Mary's hand.

"You're not in front of us, Chester. Mike and I were here first, so get at the end of the line. And quit yelling at Mary. She's not your property and she doesn't have to sit with you if she doesn't want to."

Mary's eyes grew wide, then a weak smile formed at the corners of her mouth.

"Do you want to sit with him?" I asked her.

She frowned, then shook her head.

Chester growled.

"Shut up, Chester," I said, "and let Mary talk."

"Do you want to sit with me?" I asked her.

Her eyes sparkled.

"I'd love to sit with you, Harry," she said.

So that was that.

All this time she'd been waiting for me to make the first move.

Mary wasn't a scrawny little kid anymore. She was quite beautiful. And now my crush on her was bigger than hers had ever been on me.

Mike didn't seem too upset that he wouldn't be sitting with me on the ride home now. At least he didn't have to sit with Chester. He was probably glad to see Mary get out from Chester's clutches. Mike probably wondered what had taken me so long to make a move for Mary.

Mike was also in a good mood because his father was coming home soon, too. He, his mom, and Mary hadn't seen Mike's dad since the day he'd been taken away for questioning. For the last few days, all Mike could talk about was how excited he was that his father was coming home. They had received letters from him over the years. They knew he was okay, though he didn't think he'd ever be able to buy another fishing boat. He'd probably have to find another line of work once he came home. Mike, Mary, and their mother would be staying with old friends for a few weeks until their father got back to town. After that, they didn't know where they'd end up.

By late afternoon, the bus rolled into Seven Cedars. The shades on the bus were all up this time and we could clearly see everything outside. No dust storms. Everyone talked excitedly as the bus came to a stop at Seven Cedars High School. It looked about the same as it had the day we left. We'd be staying with Mr. Mack and his family for a few days or weeks until we could find a place of our own and Papa could find a job. Mr. Mack was going to meet us at the school.

Mary and I stepped off the bus.

"Looks pretty much the same around here, doesn't it?" I said.

Mary pointed to the sidewalk. "They planted some bushes by the sidewalk. Other than that, yeah, everything looks the same."

Everyone else got off the bus. Some people simply walked away with their suitcases.

After our family said good-bye to Mike's family, they drove off with their friends. We waited for Mr. Mack to show up. Finally, he arrived in a big blue Ford.

"Welcome home," he said as he hugged each of us, one by one.

He took us to his house. That night the four of us slept in real beds for the first time in three years. It was wonderful!

After a few days, Papa said I should go back to school. It was going to be strange going back to school, especially now that I was in high school. It would be weird to see people I had not seen in three years. But I knew I had to do it. Mr. Mack dropped me off for my first day of high school. I got out of the car and walked up the steps. I'd just gotten in the door when someone poked me in the back.

I turned around.

Chester?

But it wasn't Chester. He didn't live in Seven Cedars. I was just so used to having him poke me, I'd forgotten about that.

No, it wasn't Chester.

It was Tony Rossi.

He looked about the same, only a little bigger. And a little meaner, if that were possible.

"I heard you were back," he said. "I guess they decided to let all the Japs out of jail, huh?"

I thought about the big scar on Papa's forearm. This creep's father had put it there. But I also remembered what Papa had said: "I try to avoid conflict whenever possible."

Okay. I could back off from this creep.

"Yeah, I'm back," I said. "And I need to get to class."

I turned around and walked off.

Surprisingly, some of the kids from my old class with Mrs. Gilbertson seemed glad to see me. They asked a million questions about where I'd been and what it was like. At first, I was embarrassed to tell them anything. But then I realized they were genuinely concerned about what I'd been through. Imagine that.

After my first day back at school, Mike called me at Mr. Mack's house.

"Meet me at Kramer's Lot in thirty minutes," he said.

Oh, gosh. Kramer's Lot. I hadn't thought about that place in a long time.

"Sure," I said, and hung up the phone.

I got to the field before Mike did. No one else was there. But then I felt a familiar poke in the back.

Tony Rossi.

I turned around. "Hey, Tony. What's up?"

He spit on the ground. "Not much. Just here to play baseball. How about you?"

"I'm just here to play baseball, too."

Mike arrived with his bat slung over his shoulder. "Ready to play?" He glanced at Tony. "Hey, Tony."

Tony nodded. "We still don't play baseball with Japs here in Seven Cedars," he said, as he walked off.

Mike lifted the bat like he was going to hit Tony in the back of the head with it.

"Hey, take it easy," I said. "You didn't expect Tony Rossi to change while we were gone, did you?"

Mike dropped the wooden bat to his side. "No, I guess not," he said.

"Come on, let's practice some pitches."

Soon more of Tony's friends arrived at the field. They were on the far side of the lot, so we couldn't hear what they were saying. But I saw a couple of the guys pointing at us. Tony yelled at them to get into position, so they took their places on the field.

Tony and his friends got a regular little game going. But after a while, they stopped playing and some of the guys walked over to our side of the field. I recognized a few of them. There was Mario, Tony's best friend, of course. And Jeff Walker, who pitched pretty well the last time I saw him. I didn't recognize the other guys that were with him.

Mario walked up to me. "Hey, Harry. We heard you were back in town. You know, the thing is . . . we still don't let Japs play baseball with us in Seven Cedars."

Papa's words came back to me again: "I try to avoid conflict whenever possible. But if that's not possible, I stick up for myself."

"Well, good for you, Mario," I said. I looked him straight in the eye, something I had never done before. "I'd hate to see you lose a game. So I guess you're smart not to play against any Japanese players."

Tony's friends groaned.

Mario looked at the ground. Tony pushed him. "You gonna let a stupid Jap talk to you like that?" Tony asked, pushing him forward.

I stepped up to Tony. "I don't see any stupid Japs around here, Tony."

Tony backed up a step. "Who do you think you are, Yakamato? Who do you think you're talking to?"

"I think I'm the best baseball player in Seven Cedars," I said. "And I think I'm talking to a guy who is smart enough to know he could use a great player like me on his baseball team."

Tony and Mario did not say anything for a couple of seconds. Finally, Mike broke the silence.

"So, we gonna stand here and act stupid, or are we gonna play ball?"

I nodded to Tony. "I'm ready to play. You ready to play, Tony?"

Tony didn't say anything.

"I'm ready to play," Mario said. "Come on, Tony. What do you say?"

I stood rock still. Tony had no one to back him up anymore and he knew it.

"Okay, let's play," he said finally.

After that day, Mike and I never had any trouble with Tony and his friends. We never became great pals with any of them, either. But Mike and I proved over and over again that Japanese Americans *can* play baseball. And that was all we had ever really hoped for.

the end

The Real History Behind the Story

Early in the morning on December 7, 1941, Japan launched a surprise attack on the United States military base at Pearl Harbor, Hawaii. Thousands of Americans stationed at the base lost their lives or were wounded. The next day, President Franklin D. Roosevelt announced that as a result of this attack, the United States would enter World War II immediately. After Pearl Harbor, Americans were afraid that Japan was planning a full-scale attack on the West Coast of the United States. Americans of Japanese descent living along the West Coast were seen as possible spies for the Japanese government who might commit acts of espionage or sabotage for the Japanese military.

In February 1942, President Roosevelt issued Executive Order 9066, which allowed the military to designate certain areas as "military areas" or "exclusion zones" and decide that certain people would not be allowed within these areas. Soon the entire Pacific Coast, including all of California and most of Oregon and Washington, became exclusion zones, and anyone of Japanese ancestry

President Franklin Roosevelt issued Executive Order 9066 designating certain areas as "exclusion zones." This order eventually forced thousands of Japanese Americans into internment camps.

was ordered to evacuate these zones. Those who could not afford to move inland, or had nowhere to go, were transported to assembly centers and later to internment camps called relocation centers.

Manzanar was only one of ten internment camps set up in desolate areas of the United States. Eventually, about 110,000 Japanese Americans were evacuated from their homes and sent to live in these camps. Racial bias was probably the real reason for this uprooting, more so than national security. Even orphaned infants with any Japanese blood were included in this program. These infants certainly could not have been a security threat to the United States. It was also no secret that white American farmers generally supported internment because it took away their Japanese-American competitors who lived and worked on farms all along the Pacific coast of the United States.

This photo of the Manzanar internment camp in California was taken from a guard tower. Japanese Americans had to adjust to difficult conditions in the camp.

Japanese Americans in the U.S. Army

Shortly after the attack on Pearl Harbor, Japanese-American men were categorized as "4C" (enemy alien), which meant they could not be drafted into the United States military. In early 1942, the War Department called for the removal of all soldiers of Japanese descent from active duty. The lone exception to this rule was the 100th Infantry Battalion formed in Hawaii in May 1942. These were all Japanese-American volunteers. The 100th Infantry Battalion was officially activated on June 12, 1942.

In February 1943, the government reversed its decision and approved the formation of a Japanese-American combat unit. The 442nd Regimental Combat Team of the United States Army was an Asian-American unit composed of mostly Japanese Americans. (The 100th Infantry Battalion became part of the 442nd Regiment.)

Members of the 442nd Regimental Combat Team of the U.S. Army salute the American flag upon their arrival at Camp Shelby, Mississippi, in June 1943. This unit became highly decorated during World War II.

Many of these soldiers had families in the relocation centers. The 442nd became the most highly decorated military unit in the history of the United States Armed Forces.

Living Conditions

Most of the facilities used as assembly centers or relocation camps were built quickly. Several racetracks and fairgrounds were converted into assembly centers. At the racetracks, horse stalls became rooms where families were expected to live and sleep, even though these stalls still smelled like horses and manure.

One of the biggest hardships for the people who were sent to these centers was the lack of privacy. Public latrines, with showers and toilets lined up in the middle of the room, were humiliating to adults and children alike. For the most part, these centers were overcrowded. Entire families lived in a single room with only a partition that extended halfway up the wall separating them from the other families. Meals were served in a mess hall, where people stood in long lines three times a day, often in extreme heat or cold.

Personal Losses

Many internees lost irreplaceable personal property since they were only allowed to bring what they could carry with them to the relocation centers. Many personal belongings that were placed in government storage were often stolen or destroyed.

Medical care was not the best at these relocation centers. Some people died or suffered as a result of this. A few internees were killed by military guards. James Wakasa, for instance, was killed at Topaz War Relocation Center, near the fencing that surrounded the center. Two internees were killed and others were injured in the Manzanar Riot that took place in December 1942. This riot was the most wide-scale violent incident during the entire internment period. Mostly, the internees tried to make the best of their situation.

Baseball

As early as the 1920s, Japanese-American amateur and semipro baseball leagues thrived. A few players on these teams were ready to make the move to the major leagues, but then Pearl Harbor was bombed and that changed everything. As the players were sent to relocation centers, or drafted into the army, these teams quickly disappeared. To alleviate the boredom and counter the harsh conditions in the relocation centers, internees turned to sports such as baseball.

At the Gila River Relocation Center in Arizona, players developed a year-round baseball league with thirty-two teams. George Omachi, one of the internees at Gila River, later recalled, "It was demeaning and humiliating to be incarcerated in your own country. Without baseball, camp life would have been miserable." For Omachi and

Baseball became a great distraction and activity for Japanese Americans living in internment camps. This photo shows internees playing baseball at Manzanar in 1943.

many other internees—both those who played the game and those who cheered on the players—baseball was a way to establish a sense of community and normalcy to life that was otherwise bleak and demeaning.

Compensation and Apology

Japanese and Japanese Americans who were relocated during World War II were compensated for direct property losses in 1948. In 1988, President Ronald Reagan signed legislation that apologized for the internment on behalf of the United States government, saying that government actions were based on "race prejudice, war hysteria, and a failure of political leadership." About $1.6 billion in reparations were later disbursed by the United States government to surviving internees and their heirs.

President Gerald Ford probably expressed the overall opinion about the internment on February 19, 1976, when he issued Proclamation 4417, which ended Executive Order 9066. Ford said, "We now know what we should have known then—not only was that evacuation wrong, but Japanese-Americans were and are loyal Americans."

Further Reading

Fiction

Kadohata, Cynthia. *Weedflower*. New York: Atheneum, 2006.

Patneaude, David. *Thin Wood Walls*. Boston: Houghton Mifflin, 2004.

Nonfiction

Cooper, Michael L. *Remembering Manzanar: Life in a Japanese Relocation Center*. Boston: Clarion, 2002.

Houston, James D. and Jeanne Wakatsuki Houston. *Farewell to Manzanar*. Boston: Houghton Mifflin, 2002.

Sakurai, Gail. *Japanese American Internment Camps*. Danbury, Conn.: Children's Press, 2007.

Internet Addresses

Children of the Camps—The Documentary
<http://www.pbs.org/childofcamp/>

Exploring Japanese American Internment
<http://www.asianamericanmedia.org/jainternment/>

Holt-Atherton Special Collections:
Japanese-American Internment Collections
<http://library.pacific.edu/ha/wa/Japanese-American.asp>